TOGETHER
Again

LOVE ENDURES • BOOK FOUR

SUSAN WARNER

Published by EG Publishing, 2020
First Edition. March 19, 2020

TOGETHER
Again

One

Melinda Tavers couldn't hear a single word coming out of her boss's mouth. She had already said the important part. Next month, Melinda would get her promotion to be a Vice President of the Developing Rural Projects Division. Three years ago, she had come to the company Dynamic Prints as a Team Lead, and now she was a certified Project Manager who, in thirty days, would become a VP.

She was thrilled and terrified all at the same time.

She knew what Pearla Isaacs was going to say at this meeting and had agonized over what to wear. Did she want to receive the news in business casual and then smile graciously when Pearly told her the truth? Or did she want to dress in a suit that said she was corporate and nod her head when she was told about her position, only smiling when she shook hands with Pearla, to give herself a very business-like appearance?

She took the middle road and wore a dark suit with a pink blouse so she could take her jacket off and a hint of her femininity would show. She always wanted to be approachable. It took a minute for Melinda to realize that Pearla wasn't moving her mouth anymore. The lack of motion brought her back to the present. She was so close to getting the promotion she had worked it would be a shame to be ninth and inches and then blow the promotion. Pearla Matthews had been the one to fight for Melinda, but that didn't mean Melinda was getting a free ride. Melinda had to live up to Pearla's expectations. Melinda never forgot Pearla was a member of the board of directors. She was one of the few women on the board, and the position hadn't come easily to her.

Pulling herself back to the moment, she looked at Pearla, who pushed a paper across the desk between them. Melinda took the paper and looked it over. The document was a standard hire contract. The problem was it wasn't the paperwork giving her a VP title. The glow of accomplishment started to fade, and she looked at Pearla, confused.

"It's silly, I know, but the board makes things a little more challenging when promoting to a VP or higher. You'll be assigned a mentee. You'll get them set up in the company, and that will be the last item for your packet. There is a new initiative you'll be piloting is that our managerial staff understands the grass root workers of the company. Are you ready to meet your mentee?" Pearla asked Melinda with a raised eyebrow.

What she wanted to say was, No! I don't want to meet any mentee. I put my time in, and now I want my title. However, Melinda put a smile on her face and nodded her head.

"Of course, I understand." She forced a smile on her face and pulled the paperwork closer to her as if she were really reviewing it and not stewing in her angry place at how unfair this babysitting job was.

"I haven't met the gentleman, but I hear the candidate was picked from a bowl of numbers, so it was random. You aren't the only person participating in this mentee pilot. Your mentee had to be professional and have more than five years of experience."

Melinda looked down at the copy of his employee badge ID and stopped. She was looking at the proof in front of her, but she couldn't believe her eyes.

"Yes, he is stunning to look upon. His resume is impressive. He's looking for full time. It says he worked at a consulting agency before, so he should have all of the skill sets we need, and the onboarding should be shorter."

Melinda heard the words Pearla was saying, and none of them mattered. She was looking at Calvin Matthews, thirty-six, five foot eleven, 210 lbs of a well put together gym body. Melinda didn't need to look through the file. The employee ID was only a headshot, but she knew what her ex looked like. "It was hard to forget the only man she had ever loved, especially when it was the same man she felt she had to leave." Seeing him on an employee id was the last place she expected to see him. To make matters worse, if what Pearla was saying was true, her promotion was dependent on her onboarding Calvin. She didn't know what was going on, but Melinda pasted a smile on her face and agreed.

Melinda thought about telling Pearla, and then the intercom rang, and it was time to go.

"I'll introduce you, and then you two can go on from there," Pearla nodded and then stood up and brushed her hands over her red suit. Pearla almost always wore color suits. Her hair was pulled back into a bun, and a hair dare not escape. Her skin had an alabaster glow like her namesake. None of those factors detracted from the fact that Pearla was all business. It was rumored she had given up a lot to be on the board, and sympathy wasn't her strong suit.

When she walked beside Pearla, she knew it caused more than one head to take a double-take. They were the same height, but that was all the similarity they had between them. Where Pearla had sultry almond-shaped eyes, Melinda's eyes were round like an owl's. It was her mother's favorite joke that even from birth, Melinda wanted to miss nothing, and she had the eyes that saw it all. Pearla's hair was black as night, straight and controlled. She was the epitome of calm. Melinda had a bob that was a tad too long. She could tell because the blunt cut that ended at her chin that she once had was now starting to have a little curl. That meant her hair didn't lay flat and seemed fuller and wilder next to Pearla. Where Nikita had the luminescent skin tone, Melinda had the honey-baked look that said she had just visited a tanning salon or had come from a great vacation.

When they approached the meeting room, Melinda hesitated, and Pearla took the lead. She was about to see Calvin. Calvin was the reason she was here. If she were honest, it had all started with Calvin three years ago.

Three years ago, she met Calvin and fell in love. He did everything right. He had a great career, and he was, in her opinion, one of the most attractive men she had ever met, on the inside and the outside. Yet, she battled with being good enough. She had been at a rut job for ten years. Her weight was going up and down, and being next to her true love, who seemed perfect; she wasn't ready for. After two years of marriage, she divorced him, saying she needed to work on her, but he was a great man, and she wouldn't hold him up finding happiness. That had been three years ago. She'd accomplished every goal she'd set since then, except getting this VP position, and here was Calvin.

"Mr. Matthews."

Hearing Pearla address, Calvin pulled her out of her reverie. She stepped through the door, and if she thought she would be stepping back in time, she was mistaken. The man before her was harder than the one she had left. Those were the first words that came to her mind when she saw him. His height was the same; he didn't have the gym body he had before. When she looked at the way the suit fell, he was leaner.

He must have provided the picture for the employee ID because nowhere in the photo were the hints of gray that seemed to be speckled in his hair. The gray didn't make him seem weak but smarter and more alert. The overall package was intense. When he stood up, it was as if it were one fluid motion.

He looked at Melinda, and his brown eyes held her in place as surely as if he were touching her. Then after looking at her from head to toe, he offered his hand to Pearla.

"Ms. Isaacs," he said. Melinda had to put her hand on a nearby chair to steady herself.

"This is Melinda, your mentor. She'll be your guide and liaison during your probation period."

"I'm a fortunate person, Melinda," he said and gave her a nod.

"Everyone at the company is considered an asset and is expected to add to our mission." Melinda wanted to yell, no, I take those words back. Some people shouldn't be here, and the company didn't need him to add to the mission. It had been less than five minutes in this man's presence, and she was already starting to rethink her last words. She had to get herself together. Calvin was just a man. Melinda had found her own apartment in a nice neighborhood. She'd created a budget and stuck to it, educating herself on how her retirement plans really worked. She'd researched the best company for her to work with, based on who would give her the best compensation and work-life balance. That was how she wound up at Dynamics. One person couldn't erase all of that, could they?

"Ladies, please." He gestured for them to take a seat at the cherry lacquered oblong table. When he took his seat, she could feel his gaze on her. Melinda looked up, and sure enough, he had her in his sights.

"Have you had time to read the offer and the process, which is a part of your probation here?"

"I've read every word." The words were neutral, but the effect they had on her were anything but. There were some people who thought Calvin's low tones were cold, but she knew better.

"At Dynamic, we recognize that turnover happens a lot during probation in medium-sized companies because they feel left out, excluded, or can't find their path. This program and assigning you a mentor is a way for us all to make sure we've done our parts and try to avoid parting ways." Melinda had heard this speech before. Then, it had sounded professional and reasonable. Now the same words had all sorts of double entendre in them. Melinda took a peek at Calvin and could see the words had the same effect.

He had a grin that was slowly turning up the side of his mouth. Melinda looked at his lips and thought back to the times he had held her and kissed her on the back of her neck, saying, "It's you and me. You only need to look forward because I have your back."

"I am completely onboard with the program. I think new relationships need some extra care when all parties are valued."

Melinda heard the words but she really wanted to know what he was doing here. Calvin wasn't a millionaire but he wasn't hurting for money either. He partnered in a business strategy company called Step Up.

Pearla didn't seem to be moved by Calvin at all. "Yes, we want you to understand the value we are investing in you as well. Your resume was impressive and the offer made to you wasn't cheap and the responsibilities we expect you to perform aren't small. I hope you understand what I'm saying Mr. Matthews?"

Calvin was in sensory overload looking at Melinda across the table. It had been three years. Three years or not listening to her whistle snore at night. Three years of not watching those sappy movies that she insisted on watching knowing she was going to cry. Three years not having his best friend around. He wanted to pull her into his arms when she walked through the door.

"I do understand and I'm ready," he said as he kept a side view on Melinda.

He could remember the day she ripped his heart out and asked for a divorce. He wanted to beg her to stay, to ask her what could he buy or get to make it better but she was so hurt and he loved her too much to make her stay with him and suffer.

As a partner in Step Up, a problem-solving company to help others succeed, he could solve everyone else's problem but his. So he waited. He knew now how hard it was to do that. It was usually one of the first things he told clients. Don't rush in, wait. Calvin had waited for three years and for him it was over. He wanted his wife back. When Melinda had left she talked about him being perfect and she wasn't where she needed to be. He didn't get it. He loved Melinda, not Melinda the project manager or Melinda go do this for me. He loved her snoring, crying self.

Calvin assessed the situation and realized he needed to take action. His partners had discouraged this approach but desperate times called for desperate actions. His friends had other ideas, but he would tell them all tonight his was the best. He knew it was the best because he was in the room with the woman he loved.

"Mr. Matthews—"

"Calvin, please," he said to Melinda.

"Calvin, due to your skill set your probation will be a working one."

"Meaning?"

"Meaning we will be giving you a project and evaluating you at the same time you are evaluating us," Melinda said.

"It seems like this mentor program could be a way to get low cost consulting?"

Melinda raised her eyebrow. "Our intentions are honorable, Calvin, but it wouldn't be very fair to us if we paid you, mentored you, and didn't expect you to work."

"I want full autonomy on my project."

"You'll be overseen by me."

"We'll work together. I'm sure if you've seen my resume you know I don't need oversight but I'm very open to partnership."

Pearla held up her hand. "You'll have your autonomy, but Melinda will guide you on what Dynamic work conditions entail. You two must both joint approve all ventures and will work side by side. Melinda will provide me with updates, and I'll be able to track how the project is going as well."

Calvin looked at Melinda. "Are you ready for us to be each other's shadow?" He was surprised to see Melinda straighten her back and look him in the eye.

"I don't do shadows any more, but I will be there to give you guidance," she said smartly. "So now that that is settled, please sign the document."

Calvin found himself intrigued by the way Melinda answered. Until that moment he hadn't understood that the woman before him wasn't his Melinda exactly. She was the Melinda she had gone out to become. He could see remnants of his best friend, but now he was going to have to rediscover the woman who held his heart.

He couldn't wait to get started.

Melinda told Pearla she was going to work from home for the rest of the day. She wanted to make sure all the paperwork was in place for her mentee. She was calm and composed all the way to her condominium. When she walked into her apartment, she leaned on the closed door and closed her eyes. She mentally let the morning wash over her, and she trembled when she brought up Calvin's image. He was Calvin, but not. He was still a force to be reckoned with, but she didn't feel like a leaf in the wind anymore.

She walked in and kicked off her shoes and then went to sit on her couch and pulled her pink plush peep into her arms. Oh, she knew what people would say. Why does a grown woman have a plush animal and a peep no less? The animal was the first thing she had bought after her divorce. The peep was large enough to put her head on it, and she could wrap her arms around it, just like she did when she was with Calvin.

Calvin.

She held her peep close and thought about today and him. She let herself feel all of the emotions she hadn't allowed to run amok during the meeting. He was still so intense. Time had been good to him. Words danced in her head sending thrills along her body. She stretched her neck and then looked up at her white ceiling. Calvin was anything but bland. Just saying his name made her breath hitch a little as she tried to regulate her breathing.

Just saying his name brought on memories of him saying superman would be great if he just learned to wear his underwear under his pants. It brought on a tendril of insecurity of being with someone so confident and so larger than life. Calvin always seemed like he knew what he was going to do. She remembered him saying it's only a yes or a no. I've got a fifty-fifty chance of getting it right. She thought he was so brazen and sure. Memories of how tender he could be. How considerate he was to her. Those tender moments when they ate at her favorite bakery and the seats were too small for him. The moments he held her close and said nothing, and they just breathed.

Melinda swallowed and got up to get some water. She needed something to do besides think of him. She pulled her hair back into a ponytail and opened up a bottle of water from the table. She had to think cold thoughts and clear her mind. Her cell rang, and she yelped in surprise from the interruption. When she went to the couch, she found the phone. It was Pearla.

"You haven't been answering your emails. Are you okay?"

Melinda wanted to laugh at the irony. Certainly emails would have distracted her from Calvin.

"I'm fine. I just need to review for tomorrow."

"Yes, it did seem as though you and Mr. Matthews were engaged during the meeting."

"It's to be expected with a person who comes with experiences of their own," Melinda countered. She didn't need Pearla to have any doubts about her now.

"Yes, well if you have any concerns or issues, be sure to bring them to me."

Melinda hesitated. This would be the time to say, "Mr. Mathews is my ex." Then Melinda started to rationalize. Calvin wasn't a blood relative, and she definitely didn't recommend or help him get this job. Did she think she could do this objectively?

"Pearla, if I have any reservations, I'll make sure to bring them to you. As of right now I don't see anything I can't handle."

"Good. I'll see you tomorrow."

Melinda would have responded in kind, but the only thing on the other side was the dial tone. She had just put her cell down when it went off again. She looked at the caller ID, and it said Cal. Was she ready to talk to Cal? Ready or not, she wasn't going to hide.

"Melinda Tavers," she said in her best phone voice.

"Hello, Molly."

She sat down on the couch and grabbed the peep. That man's voice was winding its way through her body like a lava trail.

"Calvin."

"Ouch! I just wanted to know if we could meet for breakfast. You know I do my to do's and checklists in the morning."

"What time works for you?" She pulled the peep closer.

"Eight is fine. Is that too early for you?"

Melinda hesitated answering him. Was he asking her to come to breakfast or to go on a date? His voice resonated through her, and for a moment she gave in to a realization. It didn't matter what he said. It would all sound like an invitation.

"I can make eight, and, Calvin, remember this is business and not history. I would appreciate if you did not call me Molly."

"Of course, you get the final word."

Melina looked up at her ceiling and felt like she had won, but she hadn't. He was a magician when it came to words.

"At the office then."

"I'll be there."

She waited for him to hang up. He didn't. She heard him on the other line, and just before she could feel herself about to say something that would shoot her in the foot later, she hung up.

She put her cell down and then laid down with her peep tightly in her arms.

Calvin was on a mission. She just needed to find out what it was.

Two

Calvin sat in the car and looked at the empty streets go by as the car traveled to the Dynamic offices. Instead of sleeping, he'd spent the night tossing and turning in his bed. His dreams all came back to one woman, and right now he wasn't sure he really knew her. When he thought about Melinda, she wasn't who he had known, but she was still someone he needed to be with.

"Cal?"

He didn't turn toward the voice. He knew when Nathan had offered to drive him to work today it wasn't just out of the goodness of his heart. "Yes, Nathan?"

Nathan had pulled up in his black sports Benz this morning. Nathan had dark hair and dazzling blue eyes that changed color depending on what he wore. More than once a woman had leaned in closer to look at those eyes and had found herself in Nathan's arms. Nathan was the perfect gentleman. A woman might fall into his arms, but she was always delivered to her door. One woman had stolen Nathan's heart and since he had turned his back on ever finding true love, instead he had resigned himself to making money.

"You do realize how crazy this is?"

"Says the man who has fallen in love and will never love another woman." Calvin said as they stopped at a light.

"Do you think you can get her to change her mind?"

Calvin sighed. "I have no idea. What I do know is I need to try."

"Well, I can tell you women are a mystery to everyone including women. You think this scheme of yours will work?"

"Tell me Nathan, what wouldn't you do to get your love back?"

"Well that was an extreme question."

"Was it? I know all of my friends have warned me not to do this. I know you all think I should just accept the status quo, but if you thought there was a sliver of a chance to get her back, would you?"

Calvin turned to Nathan to find a forlorn expression on his face. "It's true I can't imagine much would be off limits if I thought it was possible."

Calvin turned away, not wanting Nathan to know he had seen his raw pain. "Well, I think it's possible, so here I am."

"No matter my personal opinion, you know I'm here for you. In fact, all of the guys are here for you. We think you might be crazy, but we hear that's what happens to hermit millionaires," Nathan said with a laugh.

Calvin waved him off. "First, I'm not a millionaire. Second, I'm not a hermit. My name just isn't on anything, so no one has looked deep enough to know just how much money I have. You know I live a very comfortable life. According to my accountant he's trying to keep me off on several millionaire lists. If the saw me I'd be swarmed with people wanting me to invest and gold diggers who would be able to prove their sixteen year old child is mine."

Nathan laughed. "Sad but true. Well the one thing you don't have to wonder about is if Melinda is with you for your money or you. Right now she probably believes you lost the company or that it's not doing too well. So if she comes back, it'll be a love match."

Calvin looked over at a smiling Nathan.

"It's not if, my friend. We're destined, so it's when."

She was already at the office when the downstairs guard told her Calvin had arrived. She was hoping she had more time to prepare, but as usual Calvin was early. When he walked through the door, he was dressed business casual. He had on a blue shirt, tan pants, and some loafers.

"Good Morning, Melinda."

If she hadn't been listening, she wouldn't have heard that slight hitch in his voice as if he had to stop himself from calling her Molly. She had meditated for an hour, listened to her Today Will Be A Successful Day YouTube video, and drove in to the soothing tones of success. When that smile came, she batted it away with her professionalism.

"Good Morning, take a seat and let's talk." She could do this. He was no longer the center of her universe. She was the mistress of her own destiny.

"Has there been a change in the agenda?" he asked, raising his hands. "Should I call my ride back?"

"Your ride? You didn't drive yourself?"

"I live in the city, having a car isn't as important." He smiled. "It isn't a very efficient to have a car."

She could see he was having a laugh at her expense.

"That's true, so let's get down to what's important so we can both go on to use our time in more efficient way. Why are you here, Calvin?"

He walked by her and saw the spread of bagels and tea she had on a small table. "Wow you weren't even going to take me out?

"I was hoping we wouldn't need to eat," she replied. The truth of the matter was she was she didn't think she could have stomached any food this morning. All of her normal calming rituals were coming to naught against the person who was her ex. Calvin was her one way ticket to unraveling.

"I've got to make sure you're okay."

"That's where you were wrong. You don't have to make sure I'm okay because it's not your responsibility anymore. So that brings us back to the original question Why are you here, Calvin?"

"I might want the experience of working here."

"Was I that naïve when I was with you?"

"You were never naïve, Melinda, and if it seemed like I was treating you like a child, forgive me. I'll tell you why I'm here if you really want to know."

"I do."

"I'm here to see if I can still do the job of a project manager, and I'm here for us."

She waited to see if he would follow up with something else. Was he serious? She just stared at him until she saw his mouth move into a smile.

"You've got to be kidding, right?"

"No, Melinda, I'm not."

Melinda had thoughts run through her mind, and she couldn't catch any of them.

"What makes you think I want to go back?"

Calvin held his hands out to her. "We're older, time has passed. You are the amazing woman I always saw you as. I—"

Melinda held up her hand. "Stop, Calvin. The problem wasn't about what you think, but about me. You coming here and pulling this prank on my job when this is my life—"

"This is my life too, Melinda. Or whatever you call this thing I've been getting through. I'm not here to mess up your job. I'm here to ask for a chance. I didn't think you'd see me and come home with me, but I wouldn't have minded if things had gone that way. I just wasn't holding my breath."

Melinda turned away from Calvin and looked at his employment contract on her desk. She thought about how this scene would have been welcomed by her past self. The old Melinda would have been thrilled that he even thought about her to come to her job. The new Melinda knew she was worth it.

"Let's cover what's important first. Do you plan on doing the work on the project?"

"Yes."

"Good, do you think you can keep your other concerns separate?"

Melinda saw Calvin's body stiffen. "Of course"

"Well, then the other issue we will table. I like me now, Calvin."

"What did I do, Molly?"

She heard the pain in his voice and there was no way she wasn't going to respond.

"Cal, it wasn't you. It was me. I know that sounds trite, but I saw you and you always seemed to know what to do and how. I was still figuring out how to speak. When I was around you, I didn't need to speak. You took care of everything. I loved it but it also made me unsure and scared to be me, to take chances. I know none of that was you, but I just couldn't stand next to you. I was always in your shadow."

Calvin listened to Melinda, and each word was a blow to his heart. He heard her words, and he thought over the time they were together. He'd wanted the best for her, for her to know she was loved. But he'd had to show it because it had been too hard for him to say the words. Actions he could do, but not words.

He let everything sink in, and his brain started to function and look at things from all angles until he had a plan.

"You know, Molly, you were my purpose. I didn't realize you were being smothered. I think we've both gone through a period where we both needed to do some growth and introspection. I'm suggesting we get to know the new people that we are. No promises and no commitments, just the chance to see if we like who we truly are. Can we do that?"

He watched her take a step back and then cross her arms over her chest. He knew she was looking for the trap. As he watched her turn his words over and over, he had to admit this was definitely part of the new Melinda.

"No commitments and no pressure?"

"None. In fact, it might not come up at all. Remember, we'll be working on a project."

"True, but—"

Calvin could see she wanted to say yes, but there was something she was searching for in his words…

"Melinda, we'll get to know each other over again. That's all I'm asking." He watched her and saw several emotions fly across her face: doubt, curiosity, and then resolution.

"Okay, we can get to know each other, but the project comes first, my work second, and us last. Do you agree?"

"Agreed."

"Good," she said with a smile. "I've created a packet for you with all of the details. Come back in the morning with the signed papers, and I'll drive us to the site."

Calvin stopped and gave Melinda a long look.

"What?"

"Are you sure you don't want me to drive?"

He saw her frown at him and shook her head. "I don't need you to drive. I can find it just fine."

Calvin was about to explain to Melinda that she was good at a lot of things but directions wasn't one of them.

"Okay, I'll see you in the morning."

Calvin was going to show up tomorrow with his papers signed and a thermos for when they got lost.

Three

"Melinda, I don't want you to take this the wrong way, but I think that the last turn was it."

Melinda continued to drive. She was fuming inside because she thought Calvin was right. Why did people name streets Seventy-sixth Street, and then name another Seventy-sixth Road and then name another Seventy-sixth Avenue and put them all around each other? Calvin had met her at the Vision headquarters so they could go to the site together. She had started driving, and she was listening to the instructions on her phone. It was all going well until the road they needed to cross was closed due to a parade.

She heard the snap of the glove compartment being opened and closed. Then the ruffling of a map. Each noise ramped up her frustration. She began to tap her hand on the steering wheel hoping that one of the streets would be the one she needed.

"I think we need to pull over and just re-assess where we are," Calvin said.

"I'm not far. Let's keep going, and it will come to me," she replied, tight lipped.

"Okay, but I want you to know I'm here with the map to support you," he said in what seemed like to Melinda to be an all too cheerful voice.

Melinda let out a heavy sigh. "Thanks," she mumbled. She could do this. Melinda had come to the site several times. Although she had to admit that she had her phone with the instructions when she came. Today of all days for the parade and for her GPS to be unable to find an alternative path.

"Umm… I'm just saying in two blocks we should probably take a right," Calvin interjected.

"I'm good, thanks. We'll be there in ten minutes," she said in what she hoped was her most authoritative voice. She drove on, hoping to see something familiar, like the diner that was near the site or the nail salon that was really cute.

"Melinda, if you tell me which landmarks you are looking for, I can help," he said.

Why oh why did it make her dig her heels in even further that he knew what she was looking for?

"The street is coming up right there."

On the block he said to turn right she turned left. Melinda would like to believe that she did it because she saw something that said turn. She didn't know, but she needed to find the site fast. After three blocks of him being quiet, she saw a woman on the side of the road carrying groceries. She put her head out the window and beckoned the young lady.

"Excuse me, we are looking for Seventy-sixth Avenue."

The young lady smiled. "I know the roads can be crazy around here. You just made a wrong turn. At the main road you turned left instead of right. You can just turn around and go about six blocks and you'll be there."

After she closed the window, Melinda turned toward Calvin and held up one finger.

"Not one word, do you hear me? Not one single word." Finally, they arrived in front of the building where the project would take place. It was going to be an assisted living home. The building was up, but the activities, program and the capacity was still undeveloped. That was going to Calvin's part.

The building itself was a brownstone, and it was in the middle of a city block. The neighborhood was quiet and the sidewalks were clean. Every five feet there was a tree planted on the sidewalk. The cars in the neighborhood varied from sports cars to family sedans. She didn't see any junkers on the street. All of the neighboring buildings were well kept, and their front yard, if they had one without concrete, was well-manicured. It was an ideal place for an assisted living coop.

Calvin cleared his throat. "So I read the project notes. You've already decided to do the project."

"Yes."

"Then why the presentation?"

"Pearla wants you to present the idea to her and two others. This is to make sure you understand the vision and can present it to other parties when we aren't there. This position requires a lot of autonomy."

He nodded. Melinda pulled the car into an available parking spot that was a block away.

"Okay, are you ready?"

Calvin smiled. "Of course, I am. I had enough time to get in the right head space during the drive."

Melinda couldn't help but smile. "Not a single word from you, you hear me? Not a single word."

Calvin smiled and got out of the car. Melinda looked at him and she took a breath and let it out. She must have run through no less than three different emotions with him in the car. Was she fooling herself about being able to keep herself around him? She shook it off and got out of the car.

It looked like no matter what she wanted Calvin was going to be her final test on if she'd really changed or not.

Calvin had reviewed the document on the assisted living home and he was excited. It was true he'd done all of this before, but it was a new thrill to be in front of people, presenting. The fact that he was doing it for Melinda was a different feeling for him. He knew his material, but it was the first time he would be doing it in front of her. He knew the numbers and had all the research memorized so he knew he was prepared.

He walked into the room and noticed his water wasn't set up for him. Calvin smiled to himself. Yes, it had been a while since he gave a presentation and no one had done his setup. He couldn't wait to tell Nathan as he stepped out of the room into the hallway and got himself some water from the fountain.

This was what he really loved to do, suggest new ideas and read a crowd to see how receptive they were to it or not. If he were honest he also wanted to show off a bit for Melinda. It occurred to him as he was taking a drink of his water that she'd never really been with him as he was working. She would always be waiting for him afterwards or have a surprise ready for him at the house. Bringing himself back to the present he ran some numbers through his head and thought about the highlights of his presentation.

He walked back into the room and took his place at the table at the front of the room. From a side door Pearla, Melinda and an older woman who according to his packet was Tammy Casson entered. If the grey in her hair was any indication she was closer to her sixties and a representative for the group who wanted to the assisted home built. They took their seats on the benches and then Pearla nodded towards him.

"Thank you for coming," he said as he picked up the PowerPoint copies and handed each one a set so they could follow along. "It seems this is going to be a more personal presentation which is probably just as well. This is a personal subject. If you'll turn to page one." On the first page was an elderly couple holding hands on a bench looking into each other's eyes.

"I remember when the biggest concern my parents thought I would have would be if I could find someone to grow old with. Now the biggest problem seems to be where will I live much less if I find that special someone. Space is at a premium as we age. Our income goes down or levels out making mature renters look less and less attractive to landlords. Due to this situation and other contributing circumstances assisted living homes are a great alternative to the rising cost of rents. There are "homes" that mature adults can go to but they can feel more like an institution instead of a home. For adults who need little to no medical assistance we can offer Pembroke Assisted Living Coops."

He flipped his page and they did likewise.

"We can now offered assisted living in renovated brownstones. The services will be located in the nearby neighborhood and surrounding city. It will offer the best of both worlds. This will also allow residents to live in smaller groups, which means they can receive more care. It will allow them to design and make their apartments their own and also provide them with the enrichment to go out supervised within safe distances from the their home."

He went through the PowerPoint showing the growing population of mature adults. He showed how the income of the demographic could support this type of living arrangement and how insurances were slowly subsidizing this movement under value based living payments for preventive health.

"In the end it would help the surrounding area bring in more businesses that would support the mature adults and the families that visit them. It increases the security presence, as that is part of the services provided by the brownstone, and they work in conjunction with the nearby police who watch these types of facilities to ensure their safety as well."

He finished the project with timelines and costs. When he was done he gave them a minute and then Pearla stood up.

"I'm impressed with the information and the presentation," she said.

Tammy and Melinda looked at one another and then nodded. Tammy gave him a clap and a large smile. "I have to say that I was a little worried when Pearla told me last week that she was going to assign this project to one of her mentees. It has been so long in the making that I wanted only the best and it seems that I have that."

"Tammy if you'll come with me, Melinda and Calvin will clean up," Pearla said as they headed out of the room.

When they were gone Melinda brought the PowerPoint copies and gave them to him.

"That was impressive. I've never seen you present but now that I have I can see why people go along with what you want to do."

Calvin raised his brow. "I've done this a time or two. It never gets old and there are still some days people walk away and say good presentation but it's still a no go."

"Well, it's all a go today," Melinda said with a smile.

"Great. Then tomorrow you won't mind walking around town with me. We can look at some breakfast and then see how it goes?"

Melinda stepped back. "I thought we agreed—"

"We agreed to address business and get to know each other. It occurs to me I offered a lot of services from the surrounding area, but I haven't seen it. I'm not making a move on you Melinda. I'm good to my word I want to get to know you and I need to know the lay of the land."

He saw her hesitate and then nod.

"Of course. I want to stay informed." She picked up the power points and walked out of the door.

Calvin smiled. He was counting on her wanting to be know every detail. It would keep her closer to him than anything else he could do.

Four

Melinda decided to meet Calvin in front of the brownstone the next morning.

"We're walking. Are you okay with that?" she asked.

He gave her a nod. "I think I can manage to walk a bit."

The morning sun was bright but there was still a little nippiness in the air. The sky was clear and the streets were littered here and there by a homeowner sweeping the front of their brownstone or a person going to the nearest bus stop. At any rate it was a good day to walk. It gave Melinda time to think on how good her life was. How secure she felt in herself. She was where she belonged.

"So, why don't you point out the places or services that will be part of the Pembrooke?"

Melinda's first thought was, But no! Then she remembered that this was a part of her new life and that being his mentee was a part of the new her. She looked at him to make sure he was ready to walk. He was dressed in a casual shirt and dark jeans with brown work boots.

He smiled and then did a three-sixty turn. "Do I meet with your approval?"

"You'll do."

"Ladies first."

"We're going to walk down to the park down that way which should give you a decent idea of the rest of the neighborhood."

"Okay."

"The area is quiet. On both sides of the streets are residential areas. When we get to the end of this block you'll see the park."

"I see this is Seventy-sixth Road and the one behind us was Seventy-sixth Place. I get how driving around here would be confusing."

"It wasn't confusing. I would have figured it out," she mumbled. How was she supposed to show him anything? As soon as they made it around the corner they saw the park. "Let's take a seat in the park." After they took a seat Melinda went on. "Around the corner from here are a couple of stores the Pembrooke will be using like the hair salon, the massage parlor and small strip mall with different stores in it."

Calvin leaned back. "I miss doing this. I was working on contracts so much I almost never got out of the office."

"I remember," Melinda muttered.

"I think I stayed in the office so long I missed out on what was important in my life."

You'll have another opportunity to present to the community board. This is all a formality but they wanted to meet you and give their opinions and input. We agreed. We want them to feel included."

Calvin nodded. "I understand that. It's easy to do things and think as long as no one says anything we're all on the same page."

Melinda sat back and looked at him. "Okay I'll go over the line first. You're right we never discussed anything. You said charge and I followed."

"I didn't know that then but I see it now. I think it's one of the reasons that we need this get to know each other period again."

She stared at him until he met her gaze. "You think it'll matter?"

"I think that when you love someone, that love grows and changes but it doesn't die."

"Okay how do you do this 'getting to know someone' again?" she asked.

"We do the basics. I notice you don't have any jewelry on," he said.

She looked down at her bare hand. She thought about all the jewelry he used to buy for her. Every trip he found a precious stone in some new setting. "I've never really liked jewelry. When I have it on I worry about losing it or breaking it so it becomes a hindrance."

He shook his head and looked away. "I didn't know."

"You were happy giving it to me."

"Your favorite color, is it blue?"

Melinda cleared her throat. "No, actually my favorite color is rust or a rich brown. I don't like bright colors and prefer deep earth tones."

"Your favorite dessert is it still chocolate chip cookie dough?"

"Yes it is."

"Whew! I'm glad I got one. I was about to say this may not be a refresher but a first time meet."

"Calvin I don't want what we had."

"I agree."

"Then what are we doing here?"

"We are building what we want."

"What if what I want is to be alone?"

"If you truly want that, I'll respect it, but I know you won't," he said optimistically.

"And you know that because?"

"Because you want to be the best version of you there is."

"And—"

"And when we're together we bring out the best in each other. Let's get walking before you try to convince me that this won't work. Besides I've got to be on my toes. I hear the community board is interesting."

Melinda smiled. "You have no idea."

Melinda got up and they walked around the neighborhood. It was odd to be next to him and not trailing behind. He asked her questions as they went along and for once she felt as though her opinion mattered. It wasn't like old times. It was different in a way she never thought it could be.

Melinda had told Calvin to dress casual and don't bother with the power point presentation. It wasn't going to be that kind of meeting. He was used to having these kind of discussions over dinner with businessmen. During those conversations they usually brought up what their favorite charity was and asked if he wanted to join. He expected it to be similar. He was sitting outside of the room waiting to be called when Melinda showed up. She was in a green and white flowered dress. Her hair was swept up exposing the delicate line of her neck. She didn't like jewelry but she wasn't opposed to wearing some, he thought as he saw the flower earrings dangling from her earlobes.

"You were concerned about your mentee?" he asked.

Melinda gave him a strained smile. "Let's just say they don't call them the three crones for nothing."

"We are talking about three women right?"

Melinda nodded. "They're called Farah, Cleyvis and Pam."

Calvin looked at Melinda and smiled. "It can't be that bad. Haven't they agreed already? I mean we're not in some country place so this won't be so bad."

Melinda patted him on the leg. "I hope so."

Ten minutes later someone opened the door and called him in. When he looked at Melinda to see if she would come in with him the young man who had the door opened shook his head no.

Calvin was brought to a seat in front of a half circle table. On the table were three name plates starting from left to right it was Farah, Cleyvis and Pam. The women themselves were all older and well dressed. Each one watched him like a hawk. He was getting a warning sensation in his gut. Maybe Melinda hadn't been overstating the issue.

Farah spoke first. "So we already listened to your proposal and said yes. We just wanted to make sure someone with a little bit of common sense was running the project." Farah was a slender woman with short curly hair with faded highlights. She had on matching blue circular earrings and a large ring on her finger that she kept twisting like it was some kind of nervous tick.

"It's Julia's house. She was real good, when she was in her mind, that is. She could cook like no one else," said Pam. Pam had salt and pepper hair swept into a bun. Calvin could tell it was long because of how many times it was wrapped up. Pam was also on the healthy side. She was what Calvin would call pleasingly plump. "By the way you do eat food, not that powder stuff in the store but food, food right?"

Calvin smiled. "I do. I eat steak and potatoes."

Pam nodded in approval. "You know it's so important to know these things. We don't to have someone helping out who can't stand the smell of good food."

He grinned as he got a full smile from Pam.

"Well, I wanted to meet with you to see if you will be bringing good clean values to the place. Pam might be blinded by Julia's food but I know she had visitors going to her place. We want to make sure we are all vigilant about our moral standing. I was the preachers wife before he went to be with the father. I still visit members of the flock in this neighborhood. The church isn't that far away. Have you been to see it Mr. Calvin?"

Calvin almost choked on his laughter. "No, I haven't made my way throughout the neighborhood. I just came over the last two days."

Cleyvis nodded her head. "You're part of the young generation. I want to make sure we are finding people who want to go to the house every Sunday. I think if you have those thoughts in your mind then we can make sure it has the right feel of it. Don't you agree?"

"I think it won't hurt," Calvin said.

Farah cleared her throat. "Well, they've already got our money and he looks like he's been out of high school for a minute."

Cleyvis chimed in. "Oh he's been out of school. I'm wondering, do you have a wife?"

Clara giggled. "They have girlfriends now."

"A girlfriend at his age. What are you waiting for?"

Calvin had to keep a mental check of what each one said. It was like being in a game of badminton and he was the birdie.

He held up his hands and they all stopped and looked at him. For a moment it was a little alarming then he remembered they were just three ladies.

"Ladies, I can assure you that this project will be my focus and I'll work on getting it to fit in with the neighborhood. I haven't seen all of it but I want to make sure that it fits in with what's already here. I'm not trying to bring in a new element because I like the element that is currently here.

"I don't have a girlfriend so that won't be a problem. My time will be yours."

"You don't have a girlfriend! What's wrong with you?" Cleyvis asked.

"Oh, I don't think we can ask him those types of questions," Pam said.

"Psshaw, after all of that money they are asking we should be able to ask him his boxer size," Farah commented.

"There's nothing wrong. I am career orientated."

Farah fanned herself. "It means he's too selfish working on him to be bothered with a woman," she whispered to the other woman.

Calvin furrowed his brow and was about to respond when Cleyvis jumped in.

"Too bad. A money worshipper. I'm sure he must have had a good woman probably pass him by."

Calvin felt his mouth twitch as he tried to stop himself from jumping in and defending himself.

Pam smiled. "No worries. A couple of cold winters and he'll start to think about a relationship."

"I'm working on it ladies. It's just complicated," he blurted out.

All three woman sat back and gave each other looks and nods that meant nothing to him but obviously they were all satisfied.

"Good looks make some people think they have options," Farah said nodding at him sadly.

"Needs more time to really know himself. He's still young with milk around his mouth and wet behind the ears," Cleyvis declared.

"Well young man it was very good of you to stop by. We'll tell Pearla you look very competent. We think you're a bit young but she says you have good experience," Farah said.

"I didn't get a chance to talk to you about—"

"Oh he's a bit feisty isn't he?" Cleyvis said cutting him off.

Farah shook her head. "It's the age is all. They all think they have something important to say."

Pam gave him a big smile before she spoke. "You can go now." Her words were enunciated slower than normal as if he were hard of hearing. He stood up, nodded toward them, and went out the door.

Melinda stood up, and he walked past her, unclear of what had happened. He shook his head in disbelief that somehow he wasn't ever in control of the situation in that room. To make matters worse, he heard the clip clop of Melinda's heels behind him and heard the words that spurred him to his car.

"So I see the fates have left an impression on you too."

Five

Calvin made it to his car and slipped into the black Benz. Melinda saw his sure stride and knew the fates had struck again. She didn't ask. She just got into the car and he started to drive. She knew Calvin, and she knew what was coming.

"I can't believe that happened."

"Umm hmm."

"It was like I knew what we were doing and then the world twisted and who knows."

"Ah-ha"

"They just kept on talking as if I weren't even talking."

"You don't say."

When the car stopped at a light he looked over at Melinda. "You're mocking me."

Melinda desperately wanted to laugh. The fates weren't mean. They were just an institution in the neighborhood.

"I'm not mocking you. You're just to being in control and losing that is uncomfortable for you."

He looked at her a little longer and then put the car into gear and drove out of the city toward Long Island.

She knew he'd leave the boroughs to hit the highway so he could drive. When Calvin needed to think he always went driving. About thirty minutes later he spoke.

"I'm sorry Melinda. If I ever did that to you I'm—"

"Hold on there, before you bring out the flail let me tell you that any time you've taken over or made decisions for us both I agreed with them. I just wanted to be asked. The fates can be overwhelming at first. Why don't we regroup and get some food. It'll be an early lunch but I'm up for it if you are."

"I am," Calvin said and then kept driving.

Melinda cleared her throat. "Calvin, where are we going?"

"You wanted lunch. I know a place so—" He stopped and shook his head. "Ouch."

Melinda smiled. "You noticed and that's half the battle right?"

"Ugh! You don't win if you get half the battle. Where would you like to go? Do you have something in particular you want to eat?"

Melinda nodded. "I actually want a burger with some sweet potatoes fries."

"No problem. Is a diner okay?"

"That's fine."

Calvin drove off and Melinda smiled to herself. Calvin taking the time to ask her something was a novel experience. If he could make these small steps there might be hope of him growing. Growing into what, and if that would be with her, she wasn't sure but it was nice to be here with him now.

He pulled up to a diner that had seen better days. It was called the Flagship and if it was the flagship for something those days were long gone. The parking lot was small but the restaurant itself had a nautical theme. The door handles were nautical steering wheels. The carpet in the restaurant was blue and worn. The restaurant itself smelled of French fries and air freshener. When the waitress saw them she guided them to an empty booth.

As she took her seat, Melinda had to admit that she had dressed for Calvin today. The fates are a toll for anyone and she knew Calvin would be no different. She knew yesterday in the nail salon that she was prepping for Calvin. Why else would she be waiting in line to get a manicure and pedicure? It was a sign that Calvin was slowly inching back into her life. She wanted to show off her pretty toes and fingers in an unobtrusive way, and that led to her wearing open-toe sandals on a cool day. Being near him had caused her to fall into the foolishness.

A different waitress came by the table and she leaned down and hugged Calvin.

"Calvin! I'm so glad you came by. I was worried."

Calvin smiled. "No, Lucy I'm fine. I brought a friend so we could get a bite."

Melinda's curiosity was piqued. The woman whose name was Lucy had to be in her late sixties. At least her skin said that but she moved like she was still in her forties. Lucy's lipstick was a bit overdone in a garish red, but all in all, she was a slender woman who still looked attractive with a ponytail that swung like the best of the teenage girls.

Lucy turned to Melinda. "I'm sorry you have to forgive me but Calvin is such a sweet boy. When he comes by I totally forget myself." Then she gave Melinda a look over and turned back to Calvin.

"She looks like a nice girl. Is she yours or a friend's sister?"

Melinda didn't know what to think of Lucy's question. What she did know was that she wanted to hear Calvin's explanation.

"Aw Lucy this is the one that got away. I'm hoping she'll give me a second look."

Lucy turned back to Melinda and there was a bright new purpose in her brown eyes. "Well young lady let me say, Calvin is a bit overpowering in the beginning but he'll take to a firm voice and you'll never find a more faithful fellow."

"Hey I'm right here," Cal said.

"I'll remember that," Melinda said with a smile.

"So what will you be having?" Lucy asked with a smile.

"Burger and Sweet potatoe fries," Calvin answered.

Lucy leaned down patted Calvin on the shoulder and looked over at Melinda. "No matter what he says or shows he's one of the good ones."

Melinda watched her walk away and then gave Calvin a questioning look.

He pointed to Lucy's retreating back. "Oh you mean Lucy?"

"She's a bit—"

"She's a good woman, fierce as a mama bear and loyal," he said.

"I like her and it sounds like there's a story there between you two."

Calvin shrugged. "Not much. I have a connection at the unemployment office. Sometimes they find people who need a little extra help finding work. I know the man who owns this diner. He needed some help and it's out of the way. It's not a lot of business but enough to keep them going. Lucy wasn't asking for a big paycheck and it worked out."

"I learn something new about you every day Calvin."

He looked up at her and smiled. "I hope so."

Melinda sat back and looked at him. "Okay so tell me what the fates said that brought us out here?"

Shaking his head he looked at Melinda and had to blow a breath out. "It was the fact that I couldn't present my idea. They heard the beginning and then it was like I was in the room with three copies of my mother."

Melinda covered her mouth to hide the smile. Then she shifted in her seat.

"The trick is," she whispered to him, "you have to remember why you are here and not be moved by what they say. Sometimes what they say bothers you because you think it's true, but remember you are always in control. Don't give it away to someone."

Calvin sat back and looked at Melinda. "You're right but I wonder if I was a part of the experiences that taught you that."

Uncomfortable with the question, Melinda reached out her hand and covered his on the table. "We all make decisions. Some of those experiences had you in them but I have to tell you. You are so addictive when it comes to making decisions for me. It's easy to let you lead and to lose myself. At the end of the day it's about me." She gave him a pat on the hands and then sat back in the booth.

"So I have to say that I had several reasons for applying to the company and doing this."

"I'm eager to hear it," Melinda said.

"It's an up and coming company. It wasn't a direct competitor and it gave me an opportunity to show I could still work."

Melinda was grinning. "Are you saying you had some self-doubt and this is about making sure you still have it as far as business is concerned?"

"It is. I have moments when I wonder if I'm doing more harm than good at my company. If I can't do this project I'll consider what needs to be done."

"What needs to be done?"

"I'll consider stepping aside if I find my ideas aren't where they need to be. I'm responsible for the welfare of my company. I can't put my ego ahead of that."

Melinda looked at him sideways. "You'd step down?"

"I'd step aside. It's not about me. I owe it to my employees to do the best I can by them and I may not be that. So no I'm not giving up my company but I can acknowledge I need help or it needs a new face."

The conversation rambled on until the check came. Lucy had the check like it held a secret on the paper. Calvin took the check before Melinda could get a word out.

"Thank you Lucy," he said.

Lucy gave Melinda a sorrowful look. "Love he leaves a good tip. Besides back in my day women didn't pay for their meals," Lucy said.

"Thank you," Melinda said all the while looking at Calvin and the check.

Lucy tsked and looked at Melinda. "You can keep looking. He's not going to let you pay."

"Thank you for lunch. You know I could have charged it to the corporate account."

"No, thank you for talking me off of the ledge after seeing the fates."

Calvin nodded to Lucy as he left and they went to his car. They drove back in oddly comfortable silence. When they got back to the brownstone he got out of his car and walked her back to her car. As they reached her vehicle, she turned so her back was leaning against the door and he was in front of her. She extended her hand.

"Thanks—"

Then he stepped forward and kissed her on the cheek.

"Thanks for being there for me," he said in a low voice. With that he turned and walked away.

For a moment Melinda thought about yelling out 'Are you serious?' Did Mr. I'm too sexy for my shadow just give me a peck on the cheek and then walk away like he was the school nerd? Melinda was stuck between two places. On the one hand, she was upset how anticlimactic it was. On the other hand, she had to stop herself from covering the spot where he kissed her, vowing to never wash the space again.

It was true the kiss wasn't earth shattering but it did take her by surprise and gave her pleasant goose bumps. The most important thing it did was answer a question that Melinda had. Was the attraction and flame still there even after they had spent the day together? Calvin would insist the spark was still there, but she wanted to make sure they were drawn to the current versions of themselves and not the way they remembered each other to be.

So there it was. After all of this time pursuing her career, not once had she felt tempted to come off of her path for a man. The one time she felt attraction to a man it would be her ex.

Six

It was time to call in reinforcements or the truth sayer as Melinda like to think of her, Jasmine Pratford, her best friend. Jasmine showed up like a whirlwind at the bird park two blocks from Melinda's job. Every year the park was used to feature new art. However, when the art show wasn't there it was used by young couples to talk in private and the rest of the year it was used by seniors to feed the local birds.

Jasmine stopped in front of Melinda leaned down and threw her arms open. "I've arrived and so we know all things will be fixed soon or we will eat ourselves into oblivion. One way or another we will find an answer."

Melinda smiled. Jasmine was so dependable. At five foot two, she was slender with layered black and grey hair. Her skin was covered with red freckles because she loved to be out in the sun. She refused to acknowledge the random brown age spots. According to Jasmine, they were freckles that were just a bit darker than normal. There was no way she'd let Melinda own having age spots of any kind.

Jasmine had on a blue coat and black pants. She scooted closer to Melinda and gave her a nudge.

"So young lady, what you doing out here?"

Melinda smiled and reveled in the warmth of being with a friend. "Well, the reason I called you and the reason I'm in the park is because I'm thinking about Calvin."

"Ugh! Him. He was a control freak. I don't know how you made it."

Melinda looked at Jasmine's upturned nose. "What if I told you he's changed?"

Jasmine sat back and looked at Melinda. She moved Melinda's chin side to side so she could look into her eyes. "Are you seeing Calvin? Say it ain't so?"

"It's not what you think, but it is what you think and I need to go over it."

"If it's what I think and Calvin is involved, you don't need to get over it you need to get rid of him."

"Let's just say that a twist of fate has occurred and Calvin and I are working together."

"Oh, really? How did that happen? Could it have been that Mr. Manipulator found a way to get back into your life? No, it couldn't be. That would be too like the Calvin we both know," Jasmine said sarcastically.

"Jazz, if he had manipulated things because he missed me and he had changed would that matter?"

Jasmine sat back and let out a sigh. "You know I'm a sucker for a happy ending. I'm an even bigger sucker for a story where the man learns something. It gives me hope that I'll find a good man to marry one day. So I have to ask you. Do you think it's possible?"

Melinda groaned. "Why did you ask me that? I came to you looking for common sense and guidance."

"And I'll give it to you but... I'm also your friend and it would be wrong of me to tell you what I think about him and overlook what you are seeing."

"I'm not saying he's become prince charming. I am saying that I can talk to him now. I don't feel like I'm a bother anymore. We're working together and it feels nice. It feels like we're equals."

Jasmine gave her a small smile. "It looks good on you."

"What?"

"Confidence. So now that you've got a bit of spine to you, you like Calvin still. The same way or different?"

"It's not him I like per se. I like working with him. I always knew he was smart. But now I can see it in action and keep up with it, and it's different."

"You like him."

"I loved him once."

"It doesn't mean you like a person," Jasmine countered.

"Okay I like him."

"Well, I have to say he is eye candy."

Melinda rolled her eyes. "Really? Eye candy?"

Jasmine smirked. "Really you didn't notice he was hot? Did that escape your new confident eyesight?"

Holding her hands up, Melinda said, "Okay I admit I didn't overlook that he is still a handsome man. I think the fact that I can see so many facets of him and not be in awe of him means a lot. It means I can keep my sense around him and that's a huge step for me."

"You're right, it is. I'm your best friend. I'm supposed to tell you don't be like Icarus and try to do too much too soon. If you fly to close to the sun your wings may fall apart."

Melinda looked at Jasmine and took a breath. "It's true flying too close will be a definite killjoy. But not flying at all would be a life full of regret."

"I think I expected a she shed of sorts," Calvin said, looking around the open floor office of the warehouse.

"A challenge when we are renovating in a residential area is to find a base that is close to the site. We want to be in the community to foster trust, so not having a site isn't an option. But where to put it? The answer came to us that we could use the abandoned warehouses or stores in the neighborhood. We renovate them for our use. Because we leave it ready to move in for another renter, who is usually a business as well, we can receive a grant for the renovation." Melinda walked through the foyer. "I think I like this space the most because it was just one open space and we've sectioned it with false walls. We've been experimenting with using three-quarter walls. Using removable walls give the next renter more flexibility in how they want to setup their business.

He followed her through the foyer. There was a wall and on the other side were several chairs around an oblong table. On the far wall was a printer center with paper, printer and writing supplies.

Earlier that day he had left Melinda a message, saying he liked to work in the community where he was doing his projects, and asked if there was a way to get a budget to cover an office space.

When she replied they already had an accommodation set up he was pleasantly surprised. She'd invited him to meet her at the warehouse that was just five blocks from the site. He was delighted to take the tour with her.

Melinda pointed toward the conference rooms with the glass doors. Inside were two white boards that looked like they could swivel so one could write on either the front or the back of it. "This is where a lot of the hashing out of details occurs."

Calvin nodded and walked along the hallway as they passed two more conference rooms. "Seems like a lot of hashing out goes on," he said.

Melinda smiled. She beckoned him to continue following her. "We have a lot of passionate people who work here. However, if you follow me I'll show you where the true magic happens," she said.

A couple of minutes later they were in an area that doubled as the lunch room and the break room. "Coffee?" she offered.

He accepted with a nod. He took a sip tentatively. He shouldn't have been concerned that it wouldn't' be the way he liked it. Melinda had prepared it just the way he liked it whether she realized it or not. She got herself some coffee and they both took a seat.

"So you still want to work on this together?" she asked. "It's going to get a little more intense before it calms down."

"Doing this is important to me personally and professionally." He was more than ready to tackle the project. He found being on the ground floor of a project was refreshing. Having Melinda as his partner was more than he could have hoped for.

She nodded and then put her coffee cup down. "I have to be honest with you Calvin. I think during this project you may find I'm harder on you than normally because I want to make sure the client doesn't get anything less than our best, despite our relationship."

"I expected it."

Melinda smiled. "Good. I mean it's not good but I'm glad you understand. Although, as odd as it sounds, it would be a feather in my cap if I was able to make you turn tail and run."

"Not going to happen."

"Well, this will take time and you won't be able to hang out with your friends as much while the project is going on."

"All of my friends know me and understand what my priorities are."

"I guess it's good to have such understanding friends."

He gave her another look and realized her face was closed off. Her smile was no longer there. Then he thought of her words and he could see he had missed something.

"Okay, Melinda what have I missed?"

"Nothing."

"It's the nothing that says it's something."

Melinda stilled and then looked at him. "I don't want to interfere with any friends you may have made while we have been apart."

Then it hit him and he smiled. "You are beyond funny. If you wanted to know if I had a female companion that would feel some kind of way you should have asked me and I would have told you there is no one." He sat back and relaxed. If Melinda has even thought to ask, it meant that he was in a good place. "I'm sticking to my story Mel, you're it. I'm not saying I haven't looked at another woman but she's just been something that looked interesting as I walked by, not even worth talking to."

"Okay, It's none of my business but I didn't want to— Oh whatever, you know. Let's get going.

They both stood up to go and he offered his hand. For a moment he thought she wasn't going to take his hand. But when she did, he closed his hand over hers, and for a moment, it felt right.

This was just holding her hand. How long had he been hoping to have even this little contact with her? Her hands were smooth and soft. He knew when he she took her hand away his would carry the faint scent of lavender and sage on his. She still loved that brand of lotion that he had bought her when they had first met.

Just when he thought about moving his thumb over her hand she had stood up and pulled it back. Then she was turning to go. He knew he was feeling a certain kind of crazy. He was trying to win back a woman who wanted to prove she didn't need him. From all indications it was true, she didn't, but if the last couple months of sleepless nights were any hint, he needed her.

"Thank you!" Barclay Tanner said as he grabbed his portfolio. "I owe you big time."

Calvin laughed. "You already owe me big time. This is just a sprinkle on a big pile. Hurry up and get out of here."

"I didn't interrupt anything big? I know you're single, and it's rare that you go out. So if you had a date, I'd have to reschedule this—"

"Stop, and go!"

"You're sure? I'm not destroying a chance of you finding Ms. Right?" Barclay said as he stopped at the door. When Calvin waved him on he let out a big breath and ran toward the door. "If I can just make it past the traffic circle of deception, then I'll be able to make the client meet time."

"Hurry up. The later you are, the more concessions you're going to have to come up with."

"Billy is asleep and Mary will be home soon—"

Calvin waved bye-bye to Barclay who waved as he went to the door. "I think you are great no matter what everyone else says behind your back."

Calvin laughed.

Barclay ran out the door and Calvin heard the slam of car door and the engine as he pulled out the driveway.

Barclay and Mary had just gotten married. Mary was late showing a house and Barclay had a dinner with some clients. He called and Calvin agreed to come and watch their son, Billy, until Mary showed up.

Calvin walked into Billy's room. The room was done up so it looked like a night sky in the dark, and in the light it was a garden with mythical creatures. Billy slept in a corvette car bed. His hair was long and a hank of hair draped over his forehead. He had ruddy cheeks that looked as if Barclay hadn't been able to get all of the dirt off of them. Calvin was sure that Mary would have some choice words for Barclay when he returned about putting a boy who wasn't cleaned up in his bed. Calvin's mouth turned up as he thought about the longsuffering gaze Mary would give Barclay. Still Calvin seemed interested in how soundly Billy slept. He didn't worry about a thing and Calvin experienced a twinge of envy.

He hadn't thought about kids but now that he was in Melinda's life again, the idea of a child didn't seem so foreign anymore.

He'd always known that he'd need someone else to help him raise a child. He worried that he would be too strict. Calvin loved being everyone's Godfather but after he and Melinda had separated he had put the idea away from him. In a matter of weeks his thoughts had changed on the subject of children. Now when he was called upon in emergencies or last minute calls to help out, he looked at his friends' children different and wondered what a child would look like from him and Melinda.

Seven

Melinda never thought the day would come that she would be stepping into Calvin's place and it wasn't theirs. She stood outside the two-story aluminum-sided house, a cookie cutter home just like every other one on the block.

Melinda looked at the identical meticulous lawns. There wasn't one flower on any lawn. She supposed the area must be a coop of some sort. When he had sent her a text, she considered if she wanted to answer it. The first line of the text had said this is not work related. After looking at the phone for five minutes she grabbed it and read the invite that asked if she would like to come by for coffee. She could do coffee, and that was how she found herself on Calvin's doorstep.

She got ready to knock, and he opened the door.

"I'm glad you came."

"You were waiting for me?" she asked.

He shrugged. "Let's say I wasn't sure about anything until I saw you outside the door. Come in."

He moved aside and she walked in, surprised to find the floor was covered in a lavender carpet. She looked around the décor and wondered who had decorated. She looked back at Calvin to find him with a nervous laugh.

"You're looking and wondering what happened? Well, it's funny but not. You see I moved in here eight months ago and I haven't had a chance to change anything because I'm normally not here."

"Ah, so why did you want me to come here?"

He looked a little lost and then nodded as she'd asked a question only he could hear.

"So why here? The short answer would be because I didn't think you'd be comfortable going to our old apartment."

"You still have it?" she asked incredulously.

He nodded. She looked around and took a seat.

The couch was large and oversized. Melinda could have sunk into it. She could see how this might have been a family house before. She looked up at Calvin and noticed how antsy he was. He took seat in the love seat across from her. Then as if he noticed he was sitting so far away, he got up and sat next to her on the couch. He tapped his foot and let out a long breath.

"I'm starting to get concerned."

"Oh no, no," he said hurriedly. "There's nothing wrong. I know I need to do this and now that the time is here, I find I'm not as ready as I thought I was."

Melinda didn't see any coffee. So whatever it was, the subject was enough to rattle Calvin, and that meant it was serious. He had meant to dress casual. He had on a black shirt with white stripes and black jeans. He kept flexing his hands and every so often he'd run his hands through his hair. She wanted to do like she'd done in the past and run her hands over his shoulders and massage them until he calmed down. Melinda knew this wasn't the time.

"I know you said I was bossy and I want to change so…hold up. I'm going out of order," Calvin said.

"O-Kay. Where would you like to start?"

"It's not the place I want, but I think it's the best place," he said. He gave her a wry smile and then turned toward her on the couch.

"I was really lucky growing up. I had two fathers. One of them was my birth father and he was young, dumb, and the poster child for what not to be or do if you are about to be a father."

"Ouch, sorry."

Calvin smiled. "I have to tell you from all that I know he didn't think there would have been anything to be sorry about. He thought that everyone should take care of themselves. He did nothing for my mother except burden her with decisions while she was trying to raise me. Then one day he up and left. Well, he didn't just leave. He left after he had taken all of the money and the ring my mom had to buy for her own wedding. We assume he sold it. At any rate, we know he left." He turned back to Melinda. "She had no one then. No one who could help her make decisions. She had all that weight on her shoulders."

Melinda could see the scene in her mind. A young woman with a child who had been abandoned by an irresponsible con.

"So as you can guess, she was devastated. She called around, and no one knew where he had gone. She had to stop so she could take care of me. It was rough for the first eight months. When she was exhausted, she ran into my stepdad. He had seen my mom and liked her work ethic. As they got to know each other, one thing led to another, and they ended together. When they were together and he could see her income, he helped her make a budget. Eventually they decided she would stay home. She never worried again about making decisions she didn't want to. She helped my stepdad of course but it wasn't a priority. He made her life better and took the stress away from her.

Then my dad came back and when he saw the way she was living, he wanted her to pay him to stay away from me."

"What?"

Calvin shrugged. "He'd made poor decisions and needed money. He thought it was better than working. At any rate, they went to court, and my mother won."

Melinda nodded. "Your mother and you were fortunate to have your stepdad."

Calvin smiled. "We were and the example he showed me stuck with me. He taught me how to take care of those I love. He showed me how to value women."

Melinda understood that Calvin's father had taught him that taking care of people was loving them. He'd been showing his love, and she'd thought he was controlling her and suffocating her.

"I wanted to share that with you so you'd understand. I wanted you to be happy, Mel," he said looking into her eyes. "I didn't want it to be a box. I wasn't trying to make you less. I thought if I did this, you'd understand how much you mean to me."

She had to look away as the enormity of the cross communication hit her. She had to blink away tears. It meant her fear contributed to the problem. If she hadn't been so sure that he saw her as inferior maybe they would have still be together.

"I want us to be together and one day I'd like to be the father of your kids," he said. "I know it's a big jump. We're not even together, but I know if we were, you'd make an amazing parent and I'd be able to learn."

She pulled in a steady breath and cleared her throat of the emotion clogging it. "I know you'd be a good dad, Calvin."

"You say that now. Wait until you see me on this project. I know how to make schedules and hand out rules," he said with a small laugh. He gave her another look or two, and she knew she didn't have an answering smile on her face. "You would think with all of these issues I wouldn't want any kids or a family but you'd be wrong. I think you will be able to help me. I don't want to have a son who loses the woman he loves because he can't show her affection without appearing to take over her life. I want him to have a healthy relationship and that starts with me. I need to fix what's wrong between us, not just for us, but for our kids. I don't want to pass along this trait when I can put a stop to it. I believe I can fix it if you're willing to help me and give me a chance to make it better."

Melinda looked into his uncertain eyes and she was humbled by his honesty and openness. "You haven't left anything on the table."

"I've been going over us the last couple of days. I've also been going over your problem as well."

Melinda leaned back and looked at him odd. "My problem?"

"You still aren't sure about your self-confidence. If I'm your dark mountain we can help each other out."

Melinda thought about the information she had just learned. Now she understood how their situations had fed each other but she wasn't sure what Calvin wanted to do now.

"I wanted to explain to you my past and where we were today."

Melinda thought, But where does this put us today?

"First I want to thank you for coming and for listening," he said in a low voice.

"Well, I'm glad I did. It makes some things really clear."

He gave her a smile. "Clear like I'm not a total beast kind of clear?"

"I don't know, Calvin. It's a lot to process. I have to look at our whole relationship differently. On top of that, I have to be able to separate your drama from mine." Melinda stood and walked toward the door.

"Melinda?"

She turned and looked at him and gave him a small smile. "Give me some time and let me think on this," she said in a low voice.

"No worries, you know where I work."

Melinda gave him a nod and then left. She went to her vehicle and sat in the driver's seat. Knowing why something happened didn't take away from her experience, but she could see he wasn't the overbearing, insensitive person she had pegged him as. She didn't know if it mattered or not. He had spoken of tomorrow and a future. If she were honest, she'd have to say he was right. She wasn't a hundred percent in her self-confidence either. Her career was moving on, but her social life was nonexistent. She needed time to see if she could see beyond yesterday.

Eight

"I was curious when you said you didn't want to do lunch," Lane Williams said as Melinda walked into her office. Lane gave Melinda a curious smile and pulled her curly hair back into a bun. "I'm at your disposal. I've been kept in suspense for a good hour. It's an unhealthy state for me to be in. What's going on?

Melinda and Lane had met each other at a company function where they were promoting wellness of the employees. They'd hit it off right away being recent divorcees. She knew Lane was a person she could trust, but right now her world was turning upside down and she wasn't ready to take any chances.

Melinda pulled out her phone and sent Lane money via her phone app zelle. In the memo she put one time counseling.

Lane picked up her phone saw the money and then her eyes widened as she read the text. "I don't get it?"

"I need to talk to someone. It's a one-time counseling and I need to get a competent person now."

"You thought you needed to pay?" Lane said with a raised eyebrow.

"I thought I did and it's important. I mean, I know what we talk about is always between us, but for this I wanted to make sure we were both in the same frame of mind."

Lane smiled and showed her to a chair. "Stop tripping over yourself. Take a seat and let's talk. I'll tell you what I say at the beginning of every session. This conversation is between us and in doesn't live beyond these walls or our ears."

Melinda let a breath out and relaxed into a seat. She had gone to another therapist after Calvin and he had been wonderful but today she needed a little more.

"Thanks for taking me so soon," Melinda whispered.

"Okay, what's going on?"

Melinda wanted to ease into the conversation. "Calvin is back! We spoke and he confessed about how he was raised and now I'm uggghhh!!!"

Lane smiled. "O-Kay. Would you like to take that one step at a time?"

Melinda chuckled. "I needed to blurt that out. I was nervous I wouldn't be able to do it. I'm in a great place. My career is great and Calvin is back in my life."

Lane nodded. "So let's go over this as much as we can. First, I don't want to give you a pat answer. This situation deserves its due time. I wouldn't want to give you a cookie cutter answer. I think this one and done isn't the best way, but I'll give you the most responsible answer that I can right now."

"I'll take that," Melinda said.

"So what was it that had you running to me?"

"I never really asked Calvin why he acted so controlling. I always thought he knew what he was doing and he was so competent. Today we talked and I discovered the reason behind his actions, and it had nothing to do with me. I might have done him an injustice, and I think I can try again now."

Lane nodded and then said, "We are talking about Calvin Liadi, the man who lacked any sensitivity?"

"Yes," Melinda whispered.

"We are talking about the man who could make butter melt? According to you, that is."

Melinda nodded and smiled, hiding her face in her shoulder as she recollected saying that statement. "That would be the same Calvin."

"Well, I have to say I didn't think you would be open to trying again with him."

"It's Calvin. I thought I knew him, but then we talked. I mean, he talked and told me things he hadn't told me before." Melinda stood up and paced in front of Lane. "Anyway, when he finished talking, it gave me a whole new perspective on how he might have seen things. What am I doing? Is this totally crazy?"

Lane let out a breath. "As long as I've known you, you haven't exhibited any signs of mental instability. You attack your problems head on, and you don't make excuses, not even for yourself. You're an objective person who can come up with logical plans. So when you have new information and want to change course, I am confident you have a good reason. Self-esteem and self-confidence must start with you. A person can build or erode what they have inside but they are the first stop on self-esteem and self-confidence."

Melinda looked at Lane and then took a seat again. "I hear you. I know it's about my own self-worth and me being able to look inside of me and finding value. My last therapist used to ask me if I would date myself.

I thought it was the weirdest thing, but he was right and I would totally date myself."

Lane smiled. "Well, I don't know if I can sign on with the way he presented it but I agree that you should see good in yourself."

"When it comes to other people, I've made huge leaps, but when I'm with Calvin, it's all different. He wants to know if we can try again now that I understand his past. I think I should at least give him a chance."

"So why don't we start at the beginning. For a moment, forget he's Calvin."

Melinda raised her eyebrow, and Lane laughed.

"I know, I know, but work with me. If his name wasn't Calvin, would you give him the time of day?"

Melinda smiled. "Regardless of his name, he's still attractive. When I watch him work, he's knowledgeable and kind."

Lane leaned back in her chair. "It seems you already have this figured out."

"Maybe. Maybe what I really need is to manage my expectations. We might be able to start a relationship but I don't think we'll be jumping back to a marriage or anything."

"I'm not saying you should marry the man but I want you to be open to marriage should it come along. How are you going forward with Calvin?"

"I want to say yes."

"Yes to exploring what could be?"

Melinda took a deep breath and let it out. "Looking at what could be makes me so nervous. I don't want to make a mistake again. I don't want to be dumb and fall into the same old traps and—"

Lane placed her hands atop of Melinda's. "Melinda, don't borrow trouble. Your ability to think things through will be your undoing here. Be yourself and let things happen. Don't force it and be open."

Melinda nodded. She could do this. After listening to Lane she could see a path at least. She felt a little better. She would be able to tell Calvin yes. She couldn't tell him yes to how much and when, but at least it was a yes.

Lane tapped the table with her finger intruding into Melinda's thoughts.

"Melinda, stop thinking just for a few moments. You've got this. Common sense and a sense of self will get you through."

Calvin wanted Melinda enough to learn to give up control and wait. He didn't know how anyone was able to wait. Ever since he had spoken to Melinda, he had been waiting for her to get back to him. He knew he had left it open-ended, but any other guy would have told him the answer to a question the same night. Calvin was sure Melinda was running the story by multiple women, letting them vote on if she should take a chance on him or not. He'd seen the Lifetime channel once when he was looking for sports. He thought it was a team strategizing, but the scene had been a bunch of women discussing what one of them ought to do.

He had finally had it. This morning he was going to find Melinda and get an answer. All of his plans were swirling in his head when he heard the door. He went to the door reciting some possible words that he would say to Melinda. When he opened it, there stood Melinda.

She looked amazing. She was dressed in a maxi dress that had red and orange roses on it. Okay he hoped they were roses. Or maybe he should say they looked a lot like roses.

"I was just thinking about you," he said.

Melinda smiled. "I hope they were good thoughts."

"Truthfully I was running through scenarios where I could randomly walk into you and then ask you if you had made any decisions."

"Well, if it's any consolation, our last meeting was on my mind as well. I was hoping that you'd invite me in."

"Oh! Sorry, please come in," he said, motioning for her to come inside. So the house was decidedly worse. The problem was Melinda was here before the cleaning lady. He moved the laundry pile that was on the floor to the side so she could make it to the couch.

When she took a seat on the couch, Calvin went to the other end and picked up the clothes pile and put them on the floor. He tried to put it there like it weighed nothing but he could tell he hadn't really succeeded when he saw the smile growing on Melinda's face. Even then he was more than happy to be the brunt of amusement.

When he was seated, he nodded his head and leaned forward with both of his hands clasped together.

"So you were saying?"

Melinda looked around the house as if it was the first time she'd seen it. In truth it was probably the first time she hadn't seen it.

"I was saying that I've thought about it and I think we should try. I mean, we were trying before, but I think we can make time to try instead of just trying to fit it in."

Calvin sat back and the air went out of him. She had said yes. He wanted to say… He didn't know what he wanted to say. She had seen enough potential to decide to give their relationship a shot. He knew he should say something, but what could he say without making her regret her decision? Then he stopped overthinking and said the first thing that came to his mind.

"When do we start?"

Melinda coughed and laughed at the same time. The she moved over so she was sitting a little closer to him.

"I must really like you because this house is a wreck."

Calvin was waiting for some rules or something that would bust the happy high he was on and when she commented on the house he was relieved and assured. This he knew about Melinda, she was a clean freak in her own right. She always needed at least one thing in her life to be pristine and it was usually her living space.

He moved a little closer until the both of their legs were touching one another. "The real question is, is the wreck bothering you enough that you feel like randomly cleaning up any part of it?"

"Don't get happy, I was just making a comment."

He looked at her and the rest of the world just fell away. A sense of peace settled inside him. He could think of plans and ways to do things but with Melinda he was all thumbs. He needed her but he hoped she needed him as well. With her saying okay to them, he felt he had a toe on the platform to get closer to her.

She thought he was the one in control but Calvin knew she held all the power. He would do anything to make her happy. He worked to make sure he had enough money to give whatever she might ask. She never asked for much but it was there. Melinda had no idea how her smile gave him peace and made him feel like he was the king on the mountain. The day she left, explaining how he was calling the shots and too controlling, he'd been hit with a ton of bricks.

Her hand was on his thigh and she was laughing. She didn't know how he felt every finger on his thigh. How he memorized her smile and how he waited for when she was really happy. She'd have a little snort in that laugh. She'd try to cover it up but it would be there.

"Well we do need to work on a schedule, but let's see how things work out on the project," she said.

"Great," he said.

Melinda cocked her head to the side and then reached out to touch his cheek. "Hey, we've got a plan."

He nodded.

"Calvin?"

He took a breath and let it out.

"I wouldn't be completely honest with you if I didn't tell you how important this is to me. I don't want to mess it up this time."

"I think we have a better understanding so we're in a better place," she said.

Calvin wanted to express how important it was to him, for them to be in a better place. It was one of the few times he had to admit he'd pay to be out of this situation, to have Melinda back with him.

"Let's seal the deal," he said.

Melinda smiled and put out her hand.

He looked at it and raised an eyebrow. "A hand shake? Wow I'm starting farther than I thought."

He watched her process what he'd said. After seconds that seemed like eternity, she turned toward him, leaned over, and placed a kiss on his lips. She didn't rush, but just when he was remembering the softness of her lips and about to sink into the kiss, she pulled back.

"Great, now the deal is sealed and we're in business," she said.

Melinda stood up and went to his front door. Before she left, she gave him one more look.

"I'll see you at work, bright and early."

When the door shut, he fell back on to the couch. He closed his eyes and moaned to himself. He didn't know how he was going to survive this, but he was going to make it somehow.

Nine

"You're avoiding me!"

Melinda cringed as she held the phone away from her ear.

"Hello, Mom."

Melinda could hear her mother on the other side of the phone. She was walking around and every so often she would hear someone in the background saying, "Hello, Sister Parker". Melinda knew her mother's face would have the perfect penitent smile on it. She would be dressed in a knee-length demure dress and black shoes with a heel no taller than two inches.

Melinda's mom, Beatrice Parker, was a force to be reckoned with. She wasn't in anyone's face except for her child. The world saw her as the nicest person on the planet. Beatrice was seventy but she could pass for her early fifties. If you asked her she would say it was because of how devout she was to her faith. She was five-foot-nine of maternal-ness. Melinda had inherited her father's nature and her mother's look. So many people had congratulated her as she grew up on how fortunate she was to have a mother who looked so much like she did. Others would say it gave her a glimpse into her future. Certainly, looking like a parent gave you a good idea of your life path.

"Melinda, are you listening to me?"

Oh the answers that ran through Melinda's head. Of course she was listening because there would be a test later on in the conversation. If for some reason she couldn't recall the words or at the very least the gist of the conversation, then an onslaught of guilt would ensue.

"I'm listening, Mom. How are you?"

Beatrice sniffed. "Well, not that you visit me, but it appears that other people have to tell me that my daughter is cavorting with her ex."

Melinda took a seat in her office and rested her head on her chair. She kept wondering who would have sold her out. Then she thought it over and realized her best friend Jasmine would have had her weekly meet with her mom. If there was one thing all mom's knew how to do, it was extract information. Melinda knew at some point her mother would find out. She was just hoping to put it off until the last moment, like right before she and Calvin decided they wanted to be together forever again.

"I'm not cavorting. I didn't think to tell you because nothing has happened, just some talk."

"You know that man is slicker than an eel and twice as handsome. I know you are an intelligent girl, but we have to think twice when we consider if you can keep a man like Calvin's interest."

"Mom, I'm not the last option."

"Now, now, dear, don't get all ruffled. I'm not saying you are the last option at all. Besides the great one above wouldn't bless me with an ugly child. I am just saying that Calvin is in a different category. He's part of those bossy men who look good and think they can say what they want and then people fall out to give it to them."

Melinda looked at her suit and wondered why she let these conversations get to her. Her mother loved her. She knew Beatrice loved her. Raising her hadn't been an easy task. Melinda was born underweight. There were so many teachers who thought Melinda needed extra help in school and Beatrice had said no. Instead Beatrice had tutored her on the side. She had hired other tutors to help out Melinda in any area she didn't feel she could help her. She did it all after work, and never complained to Melinda about how she sacrificed for her. While other conflicts may have come up, that never did. Beatrice was very particular on what she would mention to incite guilt.

"I think that there was enough between me and Calvin that we can talk. I'm not saying that we're getting back together or anything else. What I'm saying is we are both adults and we can work with each other."

"Work with each other? I thought he was just slinking around your place. Are you telling me that lothario has found a way into your workplace? You better be careful. You know how bad that could go!"

Melinda laid her head on her desk and just let her mother go on. It wasn't long before she got to the meat of the call.

"I spoke to Sister Jamison, and she said her daughter sent her away for a cruise for her birthday. I think going on such a big boat is ridiculous if you can't swim but that's not the point."

Melinda sighed. "Did you have an idea of what you wanted to do on your birthday, Mom?"

"Oh, my birthday? It's not at a good time. I know you work all the time and that you are working on your career. I wouldn't want to impose on you while you are working."

"Mom, your birthday is on a Friday."

"Yes, I'll be a little grayer. I was thinking maybe we'd do something small."

"Small?" Melinda parroted. Melinda wasn't sure if her mom knew what small was. Sometimes she wanted to ask her if she thought King Kong was just a small gorilla.

"Yes, like a dinner. I heard about a nice steak and fish place we could go to."

"Okay."

"One of the other sisters said her children took her there and she loved it. She said it had a lot of stars so it was pretty good and it was also a part of the wheel store."

"The wheel store?"

"You mean it's a Michelin restaurant?"

"Yeah that's what I said. It's part of the wheel stores. They seemed really excited about it. I just hope they don't have grease or anything there because I want to wear my Sunday clothes."

Melinda took a breath and moaned.

"Are you okay, Melinda?"

"Yes, Mom, I'm good. Did you want me to get a reservation for your birthday?"

"Are you available?"

"Of course—"

"Well then, don't worry. I'll email you the reservation. I took care of it already. It will be great.

We'll be able to talk to one another and catch up on things."

"Of course, Mom. You know I can't wait."

Her mom hung up the phone, and Melinda just kept her head on her desk. She couldn't wait, like a man couldn't wait for his execution. She didn't know a lot, but what she did know is by the time she met her mother, she better have a story put together that would pass muster at a dinner table.

"I think we need to rethink the cost for the room," Melinda said. "We want to give good quality but that brand is out of the project's budget.

The other women at the table passed the paperwork amongst themselves. It was project review time and as VP one of Melinda's duties was to review all projects and make sure they were under budget. The meeting was being held in the brownstone kitchen on a fold out table. All the meetings were held impromptu at the sites once they were started just in case they needed to take a walk through the property.

These two had been working with Calvin on the design and furniture layout. The process was simple. They had a group together where she gave the budget and direction and they had to execute. A rustle happened in the hallway and all eyes turned to see Calvin.

"Hello, ladies. I'm sorry, I didn't mean to interrupt. I just needed to pick up my mockups."

Melinda nodded and then she looked at the women. Instead of giving him a nod and being done with it they had both transformed to high school girls. One of the women was smiling so wide Melinda thought she saw a metal crown on one of her canines. Melinda just sat back and looked at the women in a whole new light. At the same time her mother's words invaded her thoughts. When Melinda looked over at Calvin he was busy looking in a pile and wasn't even aware of the theatrics being put on for his benefit. After a few more moments of shuffling paper he found his prize and waved as he left.

Melinda cleared her throat. "Ladies, do you suppose we could get back to the project?"

The youngest one, a redhead gave Melinda a wan smile. "I know you think the color and brand are out of the budget but Calvin thought the brand was a better quality and would bring a benefit to the project. So you see why we need to keep it?"

Melinda had to really stop and choose her words before she spoke. The woman didn't realize there was a problem, but her blonde companion did when Melinda didn't answer right away. Melinda could tell she knew there was an issue the way her eyes went back and forth between the redhead and herself.

Melinda closed the file in front of her and folded her hands over it.

"Ladies, I want you to know that there was a time there were no female project managers or so few they didn't really count. Men would make the argument that women didn't really belong in this field. Do you know one of their number one excuses?" Melinda paused.

The two women shook their heads.

"Because they believed that women couldn't concentrate in a mixed environment. They thought that a woman working in a mixed environment would resort to her primary thought in life which is to find a husband. I'm sure you can hear how that is just preposterous on so many levels. We are independent women who want more than just a husband to take care of us, and we are not so shallow as to be moved by a pretty face. A pretty face today will be a withered one tomorrow."

Melinda stood up and the other women followed suit.

"So hear me. Tomorrow we will review projections again. I expect the correct brands and specifications to be in there. If they are not in there I expect a logical answer as to why not. And let me give you a hint, your ovaries being moved by a pretty face is not on the list of logical answers."

Melinda hadn't raised her voice but when she was done everyone was quiet and attentative.

"I thought we were supposed to be supportive of one another?" the redhead quipped.

"Supportive of your work, not helping the cause in getting you a ring."

Melinda got up and walked out of brownstone. When she exited the building Calvin was standing on the side of the building.

"Do you have any other suggestions you'd like to put in the plan? If you do there is a change form and I review it on Wednesdays."

Calvin nodded. "I'm sorry. That was me. I'm used to being the final decision and when I said it no one naysayed me so I put it into the plan."

"I'm not an ogre Calvin. For first time mistakes, you get a pass. Let's just keep the lines clear on who makes what decisions where."

"Well, that's going to be easy. You're making the decisions everywhere."

"What?"

"I'm just saying. You make the decisions at work and you're making the decisions after work. It's a whole new experience waiting for someone else to make a decision."

Melinda sighed. "Sometimes I wish you were a regular guy who was just slow. Then I could just say it's not worth it, or this is too complicated. You always say something to put me off kilter."

"It's not my intent, but if it's any consolation, I am as much off kilter as you."

"It's not a great consolation but I'll take it."

He closed the door behind her and then moved close enough to speak into her ear. "That's the point this time, right? For you to decide when and how we move? I'm yours, Melinda."

She looked up at him, and in that moment, the enormity of what he was doing and how much control he was giving her was almost too much.

"I'm speechless."

He stepped down the steps to the sidewalk and then stood with his hands in his pocket with his paperwork tucked under his arms.

"The strong, silent type, eh? I hear that goes over pretty well. I'll let you know," he said with a smile on his face and walked away.

Melinda looked up and down the block. She was stunned. Had that man actually said that? Then he stopped in front of the brownstone in a car. He leaned out.

"By the way, my favorite color is blue."

Melinda smiled then. "Dream on," she called back.

He shrugged. "I've got to let you know."

He drove away and she had a smile on her face and a warm glow going through her body. Yeah, that was Calvin. The stakes had just gotten higher.

She was about to get into bed when her cell phone rang. For a moment she considered not picking it up but then she looked at it and saw Calvin's name.

"Calvin?"

"So I gave it some thought. I think I need a schedule, or we need to figure out how and when we are going to work on us."

"What are you talking about?"

"I have no idea when I can and can't kiss you. I don't want to act inappropriately in front of the staff."

"So you want to put our potential relationship on a schedule," she said in a hushed voice. She hoped her voice didn't sound as weirded out as she felt. "So what kind of schedule do you suggest?"

"Well we can be flexible but I think we should make a rule to give each other a call, text or email when we want to work on our relationship. For example, let's do something tomorrow morning. We've both scheduled it off, and it would be a good time for us to do us things."

"Tomorrow?" Melinda took a breath. Had her voice come over as a squeak?

"I think it works unless you have another time. We want to jump in and get started, right? I mean, you haven't changed your mind, have you?"

The words were at the tip of her tongue. She closed her eyes and then let out a breath.

"No, I haven't changed my mind. You can come in the morning."

"Good, I'll see you then."

She hung up the phone and then laid back in her bed. A schedule. Did he really ask for a schedule? Once again her mother's words came to haunt her. Calvin was a great specimen of a man. If today's encounter with the other project managers was any indication, Calvin was indeed a prime catch. What was she thinking? Handling work was one thing but this was something else altogether. Handling Calvin was—she couldn't even think about what that was.

She'd tell him in the morning. She'd say thank you for being open. Thank him for sharing. But at the end of the day, she couldn't do it. She needed a slacker, or maybe she just needed someone who wasn't smart, good looking and wealthy? She'd explain to him that what she was looking for now was an average Joe. Someone who didn't have all of his attributes. She took a breath and let it out. Melinda nodded in her bed and then sighed.

She'd tell Calvin in the morning and he'd understand. With that, she drifted to sleep, feeling better about the coming morning and how she'd break up the potential relationship before it ever began.

Ten

Calvin was at Melinda's apartment. It looked like a two story home but he knew it was broken up into four apartments. Melinda was on the first floor. He could see the curtain at the window shift and knew she was watching him.

Calvin was okay with her looking out the window. At this point he was okay with whatever worked to get them together. He had to fight his inclination to buy flowers and candy but he couldn't stop himself from getting her a carton of coffee. He did pull on the information he knew about Melinda and coffee. He bought hazelnut flavored coffee.

He'd walked up the walkway to the door and it opened. She was in blue jeans and a blue and white striped shirt. The shirt hugged her form reminding him Melinda was big into her health as well. She was never muscular but she was lean.

"You came," she said.

Calvin was confused. "I brought myself and coffee so we would both be in a great mood." He said as he held out the coffee carton.

"I see you are really on board with this."

"I'm all in for us."

"A committed man. It's just too good to be true."

"The man or the coffee?"

"Ha ha," she said. Then he saw her fold her hands over her chest and stand up straighter. Calvin knew bad news was coming. These were Melinda's tells that she was about to do or say something that was necessary but unpleasant.

"I gave it some thought and I don't think this will work," she said.

"Are you suggesting committed men can't bring coffee? Is the concern about the commitment of the coffee? It's in the carton. It's committed."

She gave him a smile and then dropped her hands from her chest.

"No, I'm not talking about the coffee. I'm talking about me and you being together."

"Okay, this is a new one because if memory serves me correctly we were together already and I think I look the same. I mean can you see some extra fat somewhere and you feel it's disqualifying me from the relationship—"

"Calvin stop," she said as she laughed.

"Okay, hit me. I'm dying to hear how you could have come up with something from last night to this morning."

"When you say it like that it does sound odd but hear me out. If this is going to work at all we need to be able to talk to one another. We should be able to talk about anything."

Calvin nodded and then looked around. "Melinda do we need to be able to talk about anything in front of your door? I think I feel at least three pair of eyes on me."

Melinda's hand went over her mouth and she waved him in. He walked into her living room. He could see the eat-in kitchen from the door. He walked over and put the carton down.

It was like old habits took over when they were together. She went in and pulled down two cups. She also brought out a small cream and some milk for him. The both sat at the table and he poured coffee.

"Okay let's hear it," he said.

"Well the long and short of it is I think you look better than me. That's not your fault. It's my issue but it will get in the way of us being together."

Calvin had to stop and really listen to Melinda. At first he thought she was just making up some crazy excuse, but as he listened to her he could tell she believed it. For a moment he was stumped and thought she was joking. How do you tell a beautiful woman she's beautiful? He never considered her otherwise. As he waited for the punchline Calvin realized it wasn't coming. He knew how he saw her when he looked at her and she was everything he wanted inside and out. Then he had to ask her the question that was burning inside of him.

"Melinda do I make you feel anything but beautiful?"

"You?" She shook her head. "You don't understand. I'm not saying it's you but—"

Calvin moved the coffees aside and then reached for her hands.

"Melinda you are beautiful."

"Calvin—"

"Shh, listen to me. We have to learn how to trust each other but I'm a firm believer that if it's true then there should be proof."

"O-kay", Melinda said.

"So let me explain. One I know you're beautiful in a lot of different ways. You've got physical beauty. I know. That's why when you wear a dress, I wait for a wind to come by so I can see the curve of your calves. Or maybe the wind blows over you and I can see the outline of perfection. I love the way you smile. It's a full smile that leaves no doubt it's real. When you laugh so hard you snort. Physical beauty is the easy one. I mean if a person doesn't have that you can buy it. You have a beauty that is priceless."

"Priceless?" she echoed in wonder.

"Melinda, you give to people in need you don't' know. You offer to help strangers on the street who seem lost. You organized fundraisers for our friends who wanted to put their kids in a private school. You look for opportunities to be good to other people and you never bring it up or mention it. That kind of beauty is sexier than any woman's shape. It's the kind of beauty that endures. It will be with you as time goes on. It will be with you no matter where you go and it inspires everyone around you. Never doubt you are the most attractive and sexy woman in the room. Now you may want a larger audience and I can't speak for them but—"

She pulled her hand back and blinked. "Shut up and drink your coffee. So we're doing this."

"Okay, I'm going to make a rule. You know I like rules."

"Okay," she said warily.

"I think we should seal our agreements with a kiss."

"What? That is so self-serving!"

"Ouch! Are you saying you don't like to kiss me?"

"Calvin don't twist my words. Of course I like to kiss you."

"Well hear me out then. I think kissing works for me all the time and I think it will be a reminder to you that you are beautiful."

Melinda raised an eyebrow. "Just how many agreements are we going to have that it will be a reminder to me?"

Calvin laughed. "I'll try to contain myself but this is brand new for us both. We're winging it here. Your thoughts?"

He watched her roll the idea over in her head and then she nodded.

"Great!" He stood up and held out his hand for her to take. "We agree?"

She looked at his hand and then placed hers in his. When he pulled her into his embrace she stiffened. He took a step back.

"This is all for you Melinda. If you're not comfortable—"

She gave a small laugh. "It's not that, it's that I haven't been in a man's arms recently and it was new." She took a step back into his arms.

He gave a sigh of relief when she walked back into his arms. They looked into each other's eyes and his breath sped up.

"Can you feel my heart Melinda? It's working double time. I can tell you it's not the effort of standing that's doing that. It's because of the woman I have in my arms."

She looked down and he could hear her swallow.

"Ready?"

She nodded.

"So we both have to remember to breathe," he said.

"I'm breathing!"

"Oh I thought you were panting with barely controlled—"

She gave him a push. "You're hot. Be happy with that and don't push it."

"Wow, what a guy has to do to get a compliment."

She stopped and looked at him.

"You like compliments?"

Calvin smiled. "I don't want them all the time but I know I'm not the only man on the planet. I don't have a six pack and I'm not getting one so—"

"Don't worry, if you had a six-pack, we'd have to reconsider this interaction," she said with a smile.

"I'm going to kiss you, Melinda Parker," he said.

"Okay, get on with it Calvin, we don't need a project plan for this!"

He closed his eyes and leaned in. Her mouth was soft and he let his lips gently move over hers. He caught the taste of hazelnut on hip lips. He felt her hands go around his waist and her fingers dig in and pull him closer. He could feel her leaning in and in that moment he was transported back in time. Every brush across her lips was a memory. Their first kiss in the park in the rain. Their makeup kisses in front of a coffee house. His instinct was to pull her closer and deepen the kiss but he remembered this was for the long haul, and he reluctantly pulled back.

He looked down at her with her eyes still closed and her lips still wet. She was the picture of Eve in his eyes. When her eyes opened, he smiled and took his hand and ran his fingers along her hairline. Just when he was about to say something a phone rang. The ring tone was the theme from Jaws.

Melinda closed her eyes and dropped her head to Calvin's chest. Calvin was disappointed that the phone rang but he was intrigued by the tone and Melinda's reaction.

"I take it you know who it is."

"Yes, I do because I set that ring tone very recently," she moaned.

Calvin lifted her chin. "Who is it?"

"My mother," she said in a low voice.

It took everything in him to not laugh because he could see there was a story here. However the grin couldn't be contained. When Melinda saw it she leaned back.

"You don't understand. My mother and I have a unique relationship."

"So it would seem. I take it this is my cue to get going. I think we've agreed enough for the day. Besides I think you need to take care of that."

Melinda shook her head. "You've always been scared of her. Admit it."

"You remember the agreement we had when we got married. You address your family and I'll address mine. I think it's the best way and I'll follow your lead."

Melinda rolled her eyes.

"I have to ask a question though," Calvin said as he put his hand on the door and she followed behind him.

"Yes?"

Just then the phone rang again with theme song from Jaws. Both of them looked at the phone in the living room.

"So, are you another shark or the bait?"

Melinda shook her head. "I don't know. Tune in tomorrow," she said as he walked out the door.

Calvin was sitting at a makeshift table in the brownstone looking at different plans. He moved one quote to the other and he was getting nowhere.

"Oh how the mighty have fallen. I like Melinda but sitting at a card table in a brownstone that needs work? Is the budget that slim on this project? Should I lend it money?"

Calvin smiled. "No one should borrow money from you Nathan. It's like getting it from a loan shark. You think you need the cash now but the interest will kill you."

Nathan laughed. "I'm a banker. It's all above the board, and you know because we are friends I'll give you a discount on the interest rate of one half a percent."

Calvin got up and greeted Nathan. "I don't have much in the next room. I brought a coffee maker. It's not hooked up to a water source but I only use the best filtered water on sale in the neighborhood."

They both went in and Calvin got two paper cups, doubled them and poured them both a cup.

"So what brings you around here?" Calvin asked as he walked them back to the card table. When they sat down he moved the plans to the floor.

"You didn't show up for our weekly get together and the guys sent me here to check on you," Nathan said. "I figured it wouldn't take long being the project was only in one building. You would either be here or not."

"I'm here and I don't think I'll be making next week either."

"Okay, so what's going on?"

Calvin looked at Nathan and took a breath. "I have to ask you a question and I want an honest answer."

Nathan's brow furrowed. "Don't I always give you one?"

"You do but I'm about to cross a line."

"Go for it."

"Do you think Melinda is beautiful?"

Nathan stopped mid-way to sipping his coffee. He put the coffee down and then looked Calvin straight in the eye.

"I don't believe in introducing a third party to help—"

"No, not for that. I'm asking because Melinda said something and I need an objective opinion."

Nathan relaxed at the table. "Well, then yes. I wouldn't date her because I'm not a great guy but she's beautiful."

"Melinda told me she didn't think she was beautiful. You know I've always thought she's amazing. I told her so but it had me thinking."

"Thinking? You mean trying to second guess a woman's logic," Nathan told him. "Listen, I know money on every continent. I can even tell you about crypto currency if you want. There are rules upon rules upon rules. All that being said I've never been able to discern how a woman thinks."

Calvin agreed, then looked at his friend. "I don't think I'm trying to figure out women. I just want to make sure that things are good with me and Melinda. I mean if anyone would have asked me if she was beautiful I would have thought she and I would have been on the same page. It makes me wonder. If we don't agree on something I think is a given, what else is off?"

"So what is the plan? I know you want to get back together but I have to tell you this is becoming all sorts of complicated."

"I have to find a way to understand or find out what else we aren't on the same page about."

"Before you go down the twisty road, as your friend and business partner who is taking up the slack while you are here, I have to ask. Do you think this is worth it?"

"This or her?"

"Is there a difference?"

"I appreciate you as my partner picking up the slack and I'm grateful you asked as my friend. So let me answer the question. She's worth it. I know I'm about to become a worm on a hook but it seems like a small price as long as I end up with her."

Nathan chuckled. "I like Melinda but I'm of the opinion no woman is worth missing business. However, I've seen this disease hit men. What I can say is trust your gut Calvin. It's never led you wrong and it's led all of us to more money. Now I'd love to stay here and finish chatting but I've got this absentee partner and he was supposed to go to some charity and look good but he's out doing some personal stuff."

Calvin laughed and got up to walk Nathan to the door. "Thanks Nathan."

"Don't thank me. This will cost you. Just not as much. Call if you need anything."

Calvin watched Nathan go. He had made his decision and now he had to make sure he had the resources to follow through with his plan.

Eleven

May I spoil you? That was the message printed on
the card that arrived at Melinda's job. It had a number
on the back of the card and it said, Call when ready. She
left during lunch and told everyone she would be gone
for the day. Pearla had lifted her eyebrow but still had
nodded her head to go along.

Melinda called and an uber showed up. It drove her
to what looked like somewhere in Long Island. When
she got out of the car it was in front of a large
manicured lawn and a maze. The maze was straight out
of the story books. It was about ten feet high and every
so often Melinda could see there were cherry blossoms
on the hedges. She was curious beyond reason and still
she hadn't seen Calvin.

A butler came up to her and offered her arm.

"Miss, you're expected. If you could come with me?"

Melinda looked at the older gentleman and smiled.

"I'd be delighted to," Melinda replied.

The older man walked her through the maze and she
was thrilled beyond reason as she walked through. Her
anticipation kept building the longer they walked. She

would look over at her guide trying to see how he knew where to go and he gave no indication at all. Melinda thought it was the sun or maybe there were markers on the hedges or the ground but she saw nothing. Just when she was about to ask how he was managing the maze, they walked out into an opening.

It was then that she saw Calvin. He was dressed in a suit, standing next to a table set with a platter of food and two tall stem glasses. She walked over to the table and Calvin pulled back the chair for her to sit.

"I'm underdressed," she blurted out.

"You are perfect."

"I'm driving us back and neither one of us drinks so we're having sparkling water. I can upgrade it to ginger ale if you like?"

Melinda smiled. "No sparkling water is fine."

Melinda looked around and then looked back at Calvin.

"Where was the warning?" she asked.

Calvin smiled. "It was the note. It said come when you were ready."

Melinda nodded. "Touché." Normally she could appreciate Calvin's wit but today she was out of her element. She knew when she got the card that she as going to see him but she was so nervous in the car and the walk through the maze didn't help to peel off some of the nervousness either.

She knew they were going to do this and she felt so silly being nervous. Melinda had just closed two large deals in the city and she had approved a thirty million dollar project. Yet here she was fretting over meeting Calvin. She had to admit it wasn't all nervous energy of fear but it was the thought of being appreciated by him.

Their kiss had shaken her and reminded her that there were other parts to Calvin that she missed and they nourished her. The way he took a step back when he wasn't sure if she was ready was something so innately Calvin. He tried to look out for her feelings. When he kissed her and he didn't lean in and just kiss her, trying to make up for lost time. It showed restraint and thoughtfulness. Those weren't words that she would have associated with Calvin before but now she did. Now he wasn't a pretty face and a smart brain. He was all that and it was focused on her, waiting for her to give the cues on what would or wouldn't' happen. Her new sense of power made her a little nervous because she hadn't felt it before and now that she did have it, it put a new kind of responsibility and control on her.

Nothing would move or happen unless she wanted it. He gave her the power and then put her in one of the most romantic places he could find. She was pleasantly surprised by the location. When she looked at the platter she saw an assortment of mini cakes. She smiled and looked at Calvin.

"You remembered?"

Calvin smiled. "I remembered when we had less money than we do now. When we would cut up a slice of cake and say it was specially prepared by the chef for us both."

Melinda laughed as she listened to him. The memories were there. Looking at him smile and the platter brought back so many good memories she had to look away or risk him seeing the tears in her eyes. After composing herself she nodded to the platter.

"This is more than one cake," she mused.

"I got cakes that reminded me of you."

"Me?" she said curious.

"There's a German chocolate cake, because I think you are sticky and sweet at the same time."

Melinda laughed. "I'm sticky? You're the one who came up with this elaborate plan for us to try it one more time."

Calvin nodded. "Maybe, I'll give you that one."

"How big of you," she laughed.

"I've also got carrot cake. You are healthy in small doses and unassuming. Carrot cake rolls up on you and you have no idea how you've finished the whole thing."

"I'm sorry, are you calling me sneaky?"

"Not sneaky. I'm saying you are addictive."

Melinda held up her hand to stop him. "Okay let's stop while it's good. I accept that somehow I am similar to these cakes in an odd way. So on that note, let's eat."

Melinda took one and ate it. Then she watched Calvin eat a piece and she had to close her mouth as she watched him. When did it become sexy to watch a man chew? Calvin brought a new look to the whole act. He didn't take little bites. He just popped the cake bite into his mouth. Then when he chewed his lips came together almost as if he was going to give her a kiss. Next his tongue came out and got that errant bit of carrot cake.

She wanted to look away but then he swallowed and the action moved his Adam's apple which accentuated his throat and led her eyes to his shoulders in his suit.

"Melinda?"

She looked up and he was smiling. Melinda smiled back.

"Your thoughts?"

"I think this is very nice and I want to thank you for remembering about the cakes but also for bringing me to this beautiful place."

"It's not over yet."

"What else is there?" she asked.

Calvin stood up and clapped. Moments later four men came into the clearing with instruments. She looked at him and she knew her eyes were wide open with surprise.

"I didn't want you to eat and then not offer the opportunity to let it digest before the car ride back."

"I get a car ride back?" she said with a smile.

"Of course, I wouldn't want you to think I'm a schmuck."

Melinda laughed and took Calvin's hand to be pulled into his embrace.

The four men pulled out chairs and then started to play on the guitars they pulled from their backs.

Melinda wasn't sure what to do now that she was in his arms. Calvin moved slowly against her giving time to adjust and it endeared him more to her. A gentle breeze came by and it pushed them along the grass to the gentle strings of the guitar. His hand tightened on her hip to swing her around and her breathing deepened and she could feel the heat flood her cheeks.

Every couple of steps he repeated the process of swinging her around and starting the steps that swayed to and fro following the tempo of the guitar strings.

"Melinda," he whispered against her earlobe.

His voice warmed her and all at once she couldn't move, she could just feel. The way his hand was above her hip the way his breath warmed that spot right beneath her earlobe. She knew it was all up to her and she wanted to look up but she wasn't sure she was ready for what he was offering.

Then it happened, he gave her a kiss on her neck and they both stood stock still. He pulled back and looked into her eyes.

"You are more accomplished than when I met you but you are still the same warm, amazing woman who humbled me when I first met her."

His words gave her courage. She stood on her tiptoes and pulled his head down and kissed him as if he were the last man on earth. She let go of her fear and her suspicious, fatalistic nature for just a few moments and indulged. When she pulled back to look at him his eyes were opening slowly and a smile was forming on his mouth.

"I need some more time but I'll remember some other things if you'll kiss me like that again," he said.

She laughed and dropped her head so he couldn't see how red her cheeks were. "Well, I don't think I'll be able to kiss you like that again anyway."

"I had to ask," he said with a shrug.

"What do we do now?" she asked.

He leaned down and gave her a soft kiss. "Now I call that friendly uber guy and you go back."

"What?"

"I'm appreciating you Melinda, not marrying you. Unless you want to tell me something?"

She was wanted to rail at him because she wanted more but at his mention of marriage it cleared the haze and made her remember exactly what was at stake.

She smiled and smoothed her hands down the lapels of his chest.

"You're right."

"Can I record that?" he said.

"Even a clock is right twice a day." She looked around wondering how this would work and then the older gentleman appeared. He offered his arm and a smile.

"May I?" the older gentleman asked.

"Thank you so much."

Twelve

"We are very happy to see how well you have handled having a mentee," Pearla said. She looked up from her folder to Melinda. "It has come to my attention that there was a prior relationship with your mentee. I didn't interfere but I'm happy to say that it has had no visible effect on the way you treat him. I've heard that you are quick to instruct when you think he or others on the team have stepped out of line."

Melinda shifted uncomfortable in her seat. "It wasn't my intention to make him into an example. I wanted to make sure everyone understood their place in the project. It's not personal. It's about getting the project done."

"Yes everyone agreed you were project centric," one of the other partners at the table said.

"My intent is to be efficient," Melinda replied.

"No one here is saying you don't run the projects efficiently. In fact, there are several people who ask to be on your team. It appears you have a growing reputation that follows you and we are always looking for new ways to attract talent. As a result, we want to ask you if you feel you are ready to move on with another mentee. We are very interested in the results you are getting in."

Melinda looked around the able and saw the nodding heads. She was on one side of the table across from Pearl and the other partner Leila Coombs. She understood this was part of the process. Pearla had explained, to be promoted, Melinda would have these evaluations, but at this point it was just dotting the i's and crossing the t's. This and the other interview processes were just preliminaries to her becoming a partner. They went over the brownstone project. They reviewed her other successes and asked her why she deviated from the process or the norm. They went through a couple more projects. With each one they asked her to explain her thinking and the responses were met with approving nods.

Finally, they got back to her current mentee after her project review and a future plan for her to take on more mentees.

"So what is your thought on Calvin?"

"I think he adapts very well. He had a little shaky start but he has good ideas to contribute to the project," she started. "He's part of the minority when it comes to men and women but he's respectful and he's efficient."

"He was given good reviews and references from other project members," Leila added. "However we must take into account that he's not exactly a novice."

"Have you considered that he may be here to get an inside look at how we do things?" Pearla asked.

Melinda looked up at Pearla and was surprised by the question. After all of the good things they had covered she couldn't believe Pearla would bring this concern up now. Melinda wanted to be a partner but she discovered she wasn't ready to throw Calvin under the bus to do it. He should be judged by what he had done not what people thought he was doing.

"I think that Calvin has had a lot offer and that if his intentions were nefarious, I would have known by now. However, in keeping with our internal protocol he doesn't have access to our suppliers. He does his work on site. He may take some sketches home but those are filed in with the city anyway. I would like us to look at what has delivered in his daily work. Calvin is a good employee and he has a lot of patience and passion for the work."

"Please we don't think there is anything inappropriate going on but we wanted to make sure that you're comfortable in all situations. Pearla and I have discussed this and while we are very happy with the way you've been addressing the situation we think that maybe you should think about letting Calvin go within the probation period."

Melinda gave them both a second look. "Excuse me?"

Pearla's face didn't change. "Would that be a problem Melinda? I mean in the grand scheme of things I think we've already addressed that you can handle yourself. Calvin seems like an unnecessary potential complication. It's not to say he wouldn't be an asset or that you can't manage him. But why encourage the hassle?"

Melinda looked at Pearla's cool face and Leila's blank one. She couldn't believe how nonchalant they were being about someone's life and livelihood. "Are you saying you want to let him go because he might be a problem?"

Leila cleared her throat. "What we're saying is why

take the chance? You've already proven that you can handle him and we don't need him beyond that."

"I know he had his own concerns when he came to us about his own capabilities. What reason would I give him about being let go?"

Leila looked at Pearla and then Melinda. "It's an at will state. We don't have to give any reason. However, I am interested in why it seems to move you one way or another?"

"It's not because it's him. I want to make sure that anyone that I'm mentoring gets a fair chance at being a success in the company. He's not the normal candidate, but he's a good candidate. He will be a good asset to the company, and that is my concern and focus."

Pearla nodded and then looked at Leila. "Melinda is correct. It's a partner's responsibility to get new talent as well as to make judgments on the current talent. Letting him go because he has a unique history may not be in the best interest of the company in the long run."

Melinda saw Leila shift in her seat and then slightly purse her lips. She wasn't happy with the way Pearla had sided with Melinda. At least that was the impression Melinda got from the way she looked at them both. "I'll concede to the both of you on this one. However, I want to be clear that if anything happens it will be on Melinda's head and he'll have to be released immediately."

Melinda looked at Pearla who agreed and Melinda held her tongue. Leila brought up other potential mentee candidates but the whole event had Melinda wondering whether she wanted to do this. Did she really want to be a part of this group? Being partner wasn't what she thought it would be.

She was so angry she did the one thing that would help her she unobtrusively pulled out her phone and texted:

Need to meet in the bird park in 30.

"You had to be there," Melinda said as she tossed bread toward the gathering of pigeons. "I mean at any moment I expected them to jump out and say maybe he's a spy and we should out him now. I just don't get why they were acting this way."

Jasmine took some bread from Melinda hands and tried to throw them far from them both.

"What are you doing?" Melinda asked.

"I'm trying to give the less confident pigeons a chance," Jasmine said.

Melinda stopped and looked at Jasmine with a smirk on her face.

"Less confident pigeons? They are essentially flying rats."

Jasmine tsked her and waved her finger in the negative.

"You see that is where you're wrong. Pigeons are monogamous. Also, I'd like to point out that even if they were the equivalent of flying rats that doesn't negate that some rats come out right away and some hang in the shadows and wait for an opportunity."

Melinda watched Jasmine throw another handful of bread away from them.

"What was I saying?"

"You were up in arms that someone had dared to challenge the pristine intentions of your beloved one. I mean I can't imagine why they would question anything. He didn't disclose he worked in a comparable industry or that he has a personal relationship with you and now has access to company property. You're right, they are totally out of line by questioning him."

Melinda stopped and looked at Jasmine. "You're on my side right?"

Jasmine stopped throwing bread. "I am always on your side but that doesn't mean I agree with what you are doing."

"Jazz, you've never had a problem speaking your mind. What am I missing?"

"I don't know you are missing anything and that may be the problem as well. I just want you to be careful here. Everything that Calvin does you are ready to defend."

"I didn't defend him because he was Calvin. I defended him because I would have done it for any one in my ranks."

"Hey, I've known you since kindergarten. I know you are a good person and you would defend the underdog. The difference here is this dog used to call your house home."

"We've keeping our work life and play life separate."

"You have a work and a play life. Maybe you're too far gone already."

"Jazz, we're still talking over how things were."

"Then that means you're trying to fix your relationship. I'm not saying don't do it. I'm saying be careful."

"I thought I was taking it slow and being nothing but careful," Melinda replied.

"As soon as you get comfortable and you think

you've got it under control, that's your sign it's gotten away from you."

Melinda smiled and tossed out the last of the crumbs. "You sound all doom and gloom now."

"Just because it's trite doesn't make it any less true. You know I want the best for you. The woman you are now is because you worked at it. I don't want all of your hard work to be wiped away in the tsunami called Calvin."

"Part of my healing was to be able to stand up to tsunamis. If I'm going to be in a relationship with him, it has to be as a partner. Being partners with him means I need to put myself out there, and I might get hurt but I can recover from it. Being partners means taking risks."

Jasmine stood up and shivered after hearing Melinda's words.

"I hear you, but remember this. Being partners also means giving someone your trust."

Melinda stood and hugged Jasmine. While they were in an embrace Melinda whispered, "I'm stronger now. I can do this."

Jasmine pulled back. "Famous last words. Enough! I'm your friend so I'm here. I'm just saying be careful."

They parted ways and Melinda walked back to her office. Melinda knew Jasmine was only thinking of her. Jasmine wanted to make sure she could emotionally be strong. The truth of the matter was it was too late to try and claim she and Calvin weren't in a relationship. Now she had to discover if she could juggle the relationship and career while maintaining herself as a partner.

Melinda knew her mother would be late arriving at the restaurant. It was almost as if Beatrice thought when she walked into the restaurant everyone had been waiting for her arrival. Melinda grew up under the flamboyant shadow of her mother. Melinda just had to make it through the evening.

It was almost like a job interview. Melinda had studied for tonight and practiced in front of the mirror. She never understood why she couldn't have a regular relationship with her mother like other girls. However, no matter how much drama Beatrice brought Melinda knew she did it from a place of love. That was why she was in this restaurant tonight.

She waited until it was fourteen minutes past the hour and then looked up. Beatrice believed in the fifteen minute college rule. If either party was later than fifteen minutes then the meeting was off.

Melinda looked up and fourteen minutes on the dot in came Beatrice. She had on a white jump suit with a flowing tan sleeveless vest on. She had a smile on her face that made you see the dynamic woman beneath.

"I'm here. I hope I wasn't too late," Beatrice said with a voice that was a little winded. She took a seat and then looked at Melinda. "Melinda my dear you look beautiful as always."

Melinda knew her mom wasn't being mean but the comment made her reflect on her own clothing. She was dressed in business black plants and a beige top that had a large bow on the front with pearl wanna be buttons. She thought she looked conservative but then when Beatrice came in she felt like an underdressed troll.

"No mom you're fashionably late as always," Melinda said indicating a seat at the table.

"Well, I have to make sure I've done it all to look my best. It's not getting easier to look good as a woman gets older."

Melinda let that one go and waited until her mother settled in.

"The restaurant looks like it was a good place in its heyday," Beatrice said scooting up her chair. "I mean I understand the French look is vintage but these walls aren't vintage they're just old and yellow looking."

"Does that mean you don't want to eat here?" Melinda asked trying to find the calm in her soul to be able to respond in a positive manner. "If you'd like we can reschedule or I can pick another place that—"

Beatrice waved her hand to and fro. "No this is fine. Let's get started with the appetizers."

Fortunately one of the wait staff came over and took the order. Melinda used that time to regroup and face her mother. She wasn't sure when it was going to come but she knew she wouldn't have to wait long before Calvin's name came up.

Beatrice took a sigh and then it began. "Thank you for bringing me out here tonight. I want to hear all about the latest goings on in your life."

"There's nothing to tell."

"Really, Melinda, don't be shy. I heard that Calvin is back? I was surprised I didn't hear it from you, but it is what it is."

"Calvin and I happen to be working together. I didn't think you wanted to be kept abreast of who I work with."

"I do when it's Calvin. Tell me, Melinda, do you just want to keep me out of your life?"

"No, you know that isn't the case. Besides I'm not ready. I don't want to go down that road," Melinda said.

She looked at her mother across the way and never had she seemed so distant. All of Melinda's life, she had tried to be like her mother, unflappable. It was hard to want to please people and then find that you want to be unmovable and unapologetic in your opinions. The two just didn't go together.

"Did I lose you, Melinda? You seem deep in thought," Beatrice asked.

"No, I was thinking how much I admire you, and I always wanted to be you."

Beatrice gave her a smile and sat back. "I have to tell you that when you were a little girl, I was so scared I'd mess you up. You were so trusting and open. I kept thinking about how I can protect her when she welcomes everyone. Your nature reminded me that just maybe everyone on the planet wasn't an opportunistic person."

"I didn't know," Melinda confided.

"It's one of the reasons I try to keep up to date with what happens in your life. I realize being naïve maybe inspiring to others, but I don't want anyone to take advantage of you either."

"Calvin isn't taking advantage of me," Melinda said. Then the drink and courses started to arrive.

"The mimosa is perfectly mixed and the calamari was done well."

"Mom?"

"Yes, dear did you want to add to the commentary?" she said as she reached into her pocket and pulled out her phone.

"Mom, what are you doing?"

"I'm taking a picture so I can review it later."

"You do those reviews?" Melinda asked incredulously.

"Dear at my age you have a lot of time to invest into these type of things. How things look are still important to some men."

Melinda internally rolled her eyes. This was exactly what she didn't want to indulge in. "Let's get it out of the way. I'm seeing Calvin again."

"Umm hmm I know that, but thank you for finally saying it." It was as if the waiter knew all of the wrong times to bring the meal. After that statement the main course came out. The meal was eaten in silence with only the occasion accolade made toward the food. Next they decided to have coffee.

Beatrice took a sip and then looked at Melinda. She could feel the weight of her mother's gaze evaluating her.

"I know you usually only use a little lip gloss. I was wondering if this renewal of a relationship would make you consider dressing up more like a woman."

Melinda looked around the restaurant. She always thought when he mother spoke other people heard her. Out of habit, she scanned the room and found no other people looking at her and agreeing with her mother. She knew her face was pinched, and her body had tightened. She was not sure what the threat was but preparing for the attack. "One, I think I'm fine the way I am, and I'm not going to remake myself for Calvin."

"I'm not saying to remake yourself. You were always a little bit dramatic."

"Where could I have gotten that from?" Melinda murmured.

Beatrice cleared her throat. "Like I was saying. I'm not saying get plastic surgery. I'm saying a little color to the hair and maybe a little foundation and rouge on the cheeks. I'm not being critical. I'm just saying if you are going to be trying this again with Calvin, maybe he should see you like the beautiful woman I see you as. You are beautiful."

This was the crossroads that Melinda always found herself in. Her mother could deliver a backhanded compliment in a heartbeat. Melinda always felt like she couldn't respond because there was no right answer.

"I'll take it into consideration, mother. Did you want some more coffee?"

Melinda saw the frustration in her mother's eyes but couldn't do anything about it. More than anything, she just wanted this to be over. She was sure she could blink back the tears long enough to get the check and put her mom in a car.

Thirteen

"I love her so much, and I know she loves me, but she has a gift to be able to find the soft spot and then jab me with a knife," Melinda said a she picked up another sushi roll with her chopsticks. They were sitting on the floor in her living room having what Calvin called an impromptu picnic.

Calvin pushed the raw stuff to her side of the plate, and he slowly but surely pulled the cooked items closer to himself. Melinda loved Japanese food and he had planned on doing an indoor picnic with her. He knew Melinda loved the sun but hated the bugs. His options began to be seriously limited when he thought about those two items. The picnic was a great fix. He had called the guys and asked them and one of them had suggested that he shouldn't go out at all but try to recreate the setting of a picnic indoors. He had come over that afternoon with a basket and a surprise. He was met by Melinda who was feeling all weirded out after last night's dinner with her mother.

"Now I don't know if that is a gift or not. I can tell you that many a child have the same thought and experience as you. If that helps."

"I doubt they have the same experience as me. How many moms say their daughter is just not cutting it in the looks department? I think she was hoping for something else or that I would grow up to be a lot like her but that's wasn't in the cards."

"Well, I think she came out on top when I look at you."

Melinda smiled and waved her chopstick holding a cut salmon roll. "You are such a guy. Do they give you a list of guy things to say?"

"One I'd like to say thank you for noticing I'm a guy. Two the lines are my own."

"I wish for once she could just look at me and say 'you're fine the way you are' instead of 'you're fine the way you are, but I wouldn't mind making this little adjustment'."

"I hear you."

Melinda finally acknowledged the salmon roll she was waving and then she popped it into her mouth. "I know that I'm complaining up a storm about her, but I feel bad. She's only ever tried to do the best by me. It's true in a convoluted way she's always been there and been my rah rah squad."

Calvin picked up a cooked chicken tempura roll. "You are facing what all of us are facing with our parents. We want them to be there but not too there. It's funny you'd think this issue would go away when we got past twenty-five, but it just evolved."

"It seems like you've given it some thought. So, give it to me. Am I a horrible daughter for wanting her to step out of this?"

"You're not a horrible daughter. She's not a bad mom. You both should realize that neither of you are going to leave the other alone. Relationships take compromise."

"You believe in compromise in a relationship?"

Calvin held up his hands "Hey don't turn on the guy who brought food. I'll say of course I believe in compromise. I'm banking on it. So let's go over a more interesting subject than the historical trials of a mother and daughter. Let's talk about Calvin."

"Can we vote on the subject change? Besides what could we talk about?"

"Well, I'd like to know how you are doing on the job. I think it must be a huge shift for you not running everything."

"So it's humbling to not have the fist and the last word in the projects. Also, one of the things that kind of gets me is interacting with people."

"Okay, I didn't expect that one. Are you having problems?"

"I have to say this foray has made me wonder if the things I suggest get implemented because I am the boss or because they are better ideas. I never questioned that until now."

"Are you doubting yourself?"

"Doubt! I'm a seasoned CEO. I'm not doubting myself. We call it ruminating and considering all the options."

She placed her hand over her mouth to stop the laugh that was trying to burst out. "So were you ruminating on current or past projects?"

"I was ruminating on how my interactions are going."

"You know the men think you make the best decisions and the women will go along with whatever.

It's good to be you so they say. Men who follow and women who are at your feet."

"I have to tell you the women at my feet don't really do it for me," Calvin said.

"You'd be the first man I know who says women at their feet isn't enticing."

"I'm not saying it's not enticing. I'm saying that the enticement wears off after the first ten minutes and you come to your senses and realize she would be at anyone's feet she thought would care for her."

Melinda crossed her arms under her chest and looked at him over the empty containers of Japanese take out. "You know honesty is a big thing and I know I'm not the most beautiful woman on the planet. So I'm asking you were you ever tempted."

"Tempted?"

Melinda looked up and sighed. "Tempted to stray or even when we had broken up were you tempted to take a bite—"

"Let me stop you there. I want to answer this question in a very manly way. That means I'm not sure it will mean the same thing to you but it will be as clear as I can be as a man. Once upon a time I was twenty and all things female looked good. Then I became twenty-one and I realized that I had more self-control. You asked me if I was tempted to stray. The answer is no but I do find it funny for those men who haven't discovered their self-control yet, to watch them get led around by the nose."

"Oh,"

Calvin shifted and leaned over the food until they were nose to nose. "If you need further clarity I'm not seeing any one now nor did I have a regular side piece to call on. You are it." He leaned in and kissed her cheek and then ran his pointer finger under her chin and lifted her face up. Calvin loved looking at her. Her eyes were still closed and her lips were parted and waiting. This was the Melinda he missed. He loved that she was an independent woman but he still yearned for the soft Melinda that trusted him enough to be vulnerable in.

When he took his finger away Melinda slowly opened her eyes.

"We are going to make it through this to the end. We'll either be happily together or I'll be suffering."

Melinda laughed. "No pressure there."

"Yup, no pressure."

"Well speaking of pressure and timetables let's discuss today," Melinda said.

"Okay."

"The picnic counts as a date."

"This picnic?" Calvin repeated.

"Yes," she said with a smile. "I think it shows we can be friends and maybe we should include more moments like this?"

"More moments of eating Japanese food?"

Melinda gave him an exasperated look and then started to clean up the picnic he had laid out. He stood to his feet. "Let me help you."

When all of the food was up and the only remnant of the picnic was the beach towel on the ground Calvin stopped Melinda from picking it up.

"I've got that. I want to thank you for helping me out."

"I think this is a good friendly start."

"I agree, let's kiss on it," Calvin said.

Melinda took a step back. "I can't kiss you. We just ate fish. My breath will stink."

He took a step toward her and then put his finger under her chin. "If you have fishy breath then I bought you bad fish. Do you think I would buy my friend bad fish?"

Melinda gave him a smile. "No I don't, but just saying that doesn't take away my self-impression."

He lifted her chin a little more. "I'm looking at the long haul. We won't always have just brushed our teeth when we kiss."

"That is gross."

"You're stalling."

"I'm not. I'm being——"

"A scaredy cat."

"I'm not five and you can't goad me," Melinda said.

Calvin put his hands to his sides and looked into Melinda's eyes.

"Do you want to kiss me?" he said enunciated every syllable so she could smell his breath.

"Okay, Mr. Know It All. Fine, I'll kiss you.'

Calvin lifted his hands.

"No, you keep your hands to your side."

Calvin smiled and for a moment Melinda thought about taking back the statement.

"Is there anything else you want to say to me before we get the agreement kiss done?"

Melinda shook her head.

"Good"

Calvin took a step closer to Melinda. Her lips were turned up and ready to receive his kiss. He bent down, and instead of kissing her upturned lips, he detoured to her neck at the back of her ear. He didn't kiss her. He just spoke.

"If I couldn't kiss you and the only thing I could do was to inhale your scent from your neck, it would be enough."

He lifted his head and then went to the door and held it open.

Melinda was still shivering from the chills that his words sent throughout her body. When she felt the chill of the air bring her out of the stupor she was frazzled. She looked at Calvin and stopped.

"What game are you playing Calvin?"

"I'm following your rules Melinda. Since we are doing your rules I'd like to take you out tomorrow. Today's picnic was on the spot. We can do a real picnic tomorrow. Does that work for you?"

Melinda looked at him, nodded and then turned and left. She was confused and lost. She wanted Calvin. She wanted Calvin to want her. When it seemed that Calvin was giving her what she wanted, she got scared and wondered if there was any truth to her mother's words. Maybe Calvin as just in a whole different class than she was.

Fourteen

After reviewing the plans and making sure all was progressing well Melinda and Calvin decided to take advantage of the nice weather and eat lunch at the neighboring playground. It was nostalgic for Melinda to see the kids playing. It reminded her of the playgrounds her mother would take her to on Sundays. Calvin had bought sandwiches from the deli. He said it wasn't a date but it was enough down time that they could work on their relationship.

Calvin was still in his work clothes. The dress code was business casual but when he put on a shirt and some dress pants the wear looked anything but casual. Despite the frenzy of activity that had happened in the office this morning getting papers and making sure the plans, receipts and vendors were together his clothes looked as though they had just been ironed and put on his back. He looked the same way he had when he walked into the brownstone this morning.

"Melinda, come back to me," he said in a spooky, ghostly voice. "Leave work alone and try to eat."

She turned to him and smiled. "I do take breaks, you know."

"Oh yes, I'm sure you do. I think you must go to sleep at some time."

She grabbed the deli bag he had and then pulled out a sandwich for him and one for her.

"I'm going to be so avant garde here, I won't even open the bags to see what is in each one," she said to him as she wiggled her eyebrows. "It's all fancy free. You may not think this is a big deal but I work out my budget to include making extra for dinner so I can take some to work. So today, eating out like this, is a schedule blower."

"Well, then I'm suitably impressed."

"Okay, it's not that big of an accomplishment but I'm just making a point that everything isn't controlled."

He laid a hand over hers as she was opening the sandwich. "Hey, I want you to know that I am only joking."

Melinda smiled. "Thanks for not being a complete jerk."

"I have to keep you on your toes. I don't want you to get bored with me."

She gave a short laugh. "Get bored with you? That isn't something that I think will happen."

"It could happen. I have to tell you there isn't much here. I'm very what you see is what you get."

Melinda laughed. "Oh really? I don't know about that. I mean if that was true we'd have to meet twice and I'd know everything about you," she said as she took a bite out of her sandwich. She looked at the sandwich and smiled. "I hit the jackpot. It's pastrami and mozzarella cheese."

Calvin opened up his sandwich and took a bite. "Jackpot? No, but you are the recipient of my amazing planning. I remembered you liked pastrami and cheese. So I ordered two of them."

"Sure, that's the action of a simple person."

"I'm not going to let you goad me into anything. Since you seem determined to find something about me that is unattractive why don't you share something that may be unattractive about you so I'll feel secure sharing?"

Melinda paused and then gave him another look. "Well, I would tell you something, but as it turns out, all of my pieces are just right. I mean even the things that might be considered unattractive are attractive in my package."

Calvin bent over laughing. "That is definitely a new response from you. I remember you would have given me a dissertation that I had to refute about what was wrong or not attractive about you."

"And?"

Calvin smiled. "I think I like this evolved Melinda already."

Sitting in the park, watching mothers bring their children to play had a calming effect on Melinda. The gentle swaying of trees hinted at some windiness, but all in all, it was a good day. Melinda was with Calvin and they were in a place of peace. She could look at the families around her and when she would have once looked on them with envy, today she looked on at them saw hope and possibility.

She was falling into the comfort of being around Calvin. It didn't feel the same way it had in the past. Today she felt like she was an equal and there was a new easiness being with Calvin. This new Calvin shared his feelings with her. He was funny and charismatic but considerate.

She looked over to her side and saw Calvin biting into his sandwich. She thought how far she had come that she could sit here with him. In the beginning she would have been looking around the park to make sure no one from the project saw them. But now, if everyone were to discover they were together, she had the confidence to face them. Despite what Leila and Pearla thought she knew she was pushing Calvin a little harder than she would another mentee. Calvin had the chops and experience to be able to manage this job. He was actually turning out to be the best option for this assignment. It gave her faith that things worked themselves out in the end.

"Hey, have I lost you?"

Melinda smiled and looked at him. "What? Are you concerned you're getting boring?" she teased.

"Why, hello, Melinda and Calvin," the redheaded woman said.

Melinda noted there was no threatening music or anything else that signaled her coming. Certainly when villains came to the children's playground there had to be a warning. That was a rule, right? Instead, Melinda looked up from her sandwich to see the woman she had released from the project who had decided to follow Calvin despite the plan and direct orders she was given.

"Hello, Patricia, is it?"

Calvin looked up and gave her a nod. "Patricia." Then he went back to eating his sandwich. In that moment Melinda was proud of him and admired him. That he could snub a person so effectively without being outright rude.

Patricia looked at them both and a sneer marred her oval face. She wasn't an unattractive woman. Melinda could acknowledge her red hair and small frame of five foot was an appealing package. She gave Melinda a once over and then turned her attention to Calvin. Melinda wasn't surprised Calvin was her original intent any way.

"Calvin, I'm surprised you think you need to do these type of things. I mean we all want to be in good with the boss but you're really talented."

Melinda pulled a piece of her sandwich off and chewed it. If she chewed on the sandwich then she couldn't lunge at Patricia. When she had finished chewing she looked at the smirking Patricia. "I didn't know you felt so threatened by me Patricia. If you had come and spoken to me we could have worked on your issues."

"That could be the only reason," Patricia implored Calvin. "She was threatened by your new ideas, right?"

Melinda thought Calvin was going to let it go but then he packed his sandwich and gave Patricia his attention.

"She heard my ideas and gave me feedback. I don't remember you having any ideas to contribute to the project."

Patricia took a step back as if she had been pushed. "I knew she wasn't going to listen to any of my ideas," she said stammering.

"Managers don't tend to give the time of day to ideas that aren't helpful to the project."

Patricia folded her hands over her chest and started to breathe heavily before she answered. "I had ideas to share!"

Melinda looked at the interaction and she learned so much. She was caught up in the notion that he had not once raised his voice or said anything that he could be brought up on charges for. His voice was neutral and it seemed to captivate Patricia into not becoming irate.

"Why are you really here Patricia?" Calvin asked.

Patricia clenched her jaw and narrowed her gaze. "Why does it matter why I'm here? Have you two become so close that you are her knight in shining armor now?"

"You already know who I am and what my role is on this project. If I can I want to help you and that is what everyone here really wants to walk away with. So tell me what is it that you came for?"

Melinda looked at Patricia and in that moment she realized Calvin was right. Despite everything and the random false accusation, if she could, she would help Patricia.

Patricia tossed her hair over her shoulder and let out a huge sigh. "I came to talk to you, Calvin. I thought after we had gone out before you were a friend I could count on."

Calvin put the sandwich on the bench next to him and opened his arms.

"Enough, Patricia. I don't know what your aim is but I try to get to know all of my teammates. That you stayed the longest at the invite I gave to everyone doesn't mean a thing. I could see then you might be a little insecure being around Melinda."

Melinda turned to look at Calvin. At that moment she was floored that he had even said she could make anyone insecure. It was odd that he saw her as so confident, and even if he didn't and he was just doing this for Patricia, she thought he still needed a pat on the back. He was being considerate to all parties involved…

Patricia looked at them both and then she started nodding her head. After that a grin broke out across her face and then she held up both hands.

"I get it, I get it. I had this right the first time. You're not looking to run some small project you are going for the long haul."

"The long haul?" Calvin echoed in a silent voice that sent bells off with Melinda. She couldn't understand how Patricia could be so blind to the changes in Calvin. His voice was colder and his words more deliberate. Instead of leaning forward with his hands out he was sitting back watching her like a cat about to pounce.

"You and Melinda. I'm like, okay, you've got the looks. She is an up-and-coming partner, so I get it."

Melinda knew where Patricia was going, but she had hoped she would stop short of saying it. It was so odd. Even though she knew Calvin had no complaints when it came to her being ambitious, the only thing Melinda could hear was her mother's words coming back to haunt her. Those words of not being enough swirled around her brain like a wraith that wouldn't go away.

"You know what's wrong, Patricia? You missed all of the opportunities in front of you," Calvin said. He reached over and grabbed Melinda's free hand. "Melinda is the type of manager that would have taken you under her wing. She would have guided you to another project if you needed it. She the manager that might let someone go but gives them good references to help them along. You missed that. Melinda the woman is everything a man looks for. She's kind and compassionate. She thinks people are more important than stuff, and she gives unconditionally. On top of all of that, she's not moved by my looks or my money. She's the kind of woman where you know if she stays, she's with you for you and not your possessions. I'm sorry you missed out on those benefits from her. You literally walked away from a gift."

Melinda was looking at Calvin, and she wanted to be in a relationship with herself after that speech. The words were for Patricia but they were well said. Melinda wanted to believe them so badly she didn't know what to do. Instead she turned to Patricia hoping to give herself time to regroup from the declaration. What she found was an angry woman glaring at her.

"Men lie most of the time, but I hope you both get what you deserve. Good bye."

Patricia turned and went away and took everything with her. Melinda looked up and the kids were gone. She and Calvin were the only two in the park. The silence of the moment made her speak up.

"Wow," she said.

"It wasn't a problem because it was the truth." He said as he reached for her sandwich and put it on the side of him on the bench. "You know you really are amazing."

"I'm a product of my life to date."

"Patricia is jealous."

"Really, don't tell me that," Melinda said incredulously.

"Why not?"

Melinda sighed. "If you say that, then I will start to feel bad for her and think maybe I should have done more for her. Or maybe I missed the signs and should have helped her. Patricia was wrong in her approach and what she said. I know what it feels like to be so insecure that you see conspiracies everywhere, and you worry people are joining forces behind your back because they can see the weakness you can't hide. I wouldn't have addressed it the way she did, but if you tell me she's jealous, I'll know it's just fear, and I'll feel bad for her."

Calvin pulled her closer and put her hands in his. He brought her hands to his mouth and kissed each knuckle as if they were a gift. When he was done he looked up and caught her gaze.

"Melinda, look at me," he whispered.

She looked up slowly falling into his gaze.

"Listen to me Mel. You're not that woman," he said to her. "You're powerful. You're a force of nature. You may have doubted yourself at one time but you pulled yourself up by the bootstraps and molded yourself into this amazing woman.

You have the strength to stand up to me and anyone else who comes your way. You interact with people who seek you out. I'm so proud of you. I'm sorry that I couldn't be what you needed when we were together but I'm awed by the woman you are now despite anything else that may have happened. I'm honored to be with you on this bench. I am getting massive man points for being with a smart and hot woman," he said with a grin.

Melinda smiled.

"I want you to know that my woman points are going up massively as well," she said through her laughter.

"And not to be the downer but she is jealous."

Melinda hung her head. "Ugh! You know I've got to do something for her. I'm trying so hard to hang on to her accusation that you are with me to get a better position."

"I have to tell you my feelings were hurt. Is my work that bad?"

She lifted her head and gave him a look of disbelief.

"Really? As if you need any more help boosting that ego of yours."

"Mel, you're going to do what you think is best."

Melinda gave him a smile and he gave her back her hands. Calvin cleaned up and Melinda looked at him as they went back to the brownstone. Today was a lot of firsts. Calvin had stood up for her in and said how much he was proud of her. He was clear if his words were to be believed that he was ready to move into a relationship with the healed woman she was. She knew the portrait he painted was her most of the time. She just needed to make sure it was her state enough of the time to be with Calvin.

Fifteen

Calvin stared at the project plans on the table. He got up and walked through the brownstone. The brownstone had wooden floors that had been waxed and shone to perfection. There was a foyer with a hanging rack and shoe racks on the side. The foyer led to a common room and a large kitchen with an island and all new appliances. Upstairs, the individual rooms all had their own bathrooms included.

Earlier today Melinda had gathered the team in the brownstone and congratulated everyone on their efforts to get the job done. Calvin had helped her hand out bonuses and they had ordered in food to christen the brownstone. As they were cleaning up, Melinda turned to him.

"Calvin would you hang around a bit?" she asked.

"No problem."

Calvin knew what was coming. He wasn't sure how she was going to deliver the bad news but he knew. All day Melinda had made sure they weren't in the same room with each other alone. When he asked her a question, she gave him quick, one-word responses and didn't even bother to look at him when she delivered the answers. He didn't have to be a genius to understand what was going on or what was going to happen. When she asked him to hang around after ignoring him all day, it confirmed his thoughts.

When everyone was gone, she met him in the common room. She had her purse on her shoulder and she was holding onto it like it was a lifeline. He didn't know how much she would say or what she would say, but no matter what, he would listen.

Melinda let out a big sigh. "I want you to know that you've done an amazing job," she started. "As a mentee you are great and even with us working out the past."

Calvin forced his lips into a smile that he used for business but he knew didn't make it to his eyes. "I have no regrets."

She nodded and held on to her strap a little harder with both hands. He could see her teeth clenching and she was starting to fidget.

"Well, that's what I want to talk about. I think now that this project is over we should part ways. I can get you another mentor and then we won't have to do the meet thing either."

He angled his head to catch her gaze. "You made this decision when?"

"It doesn't matter when I made the decision. What matters is I think this is the best thing for us."

"Really?"

Anger was ripping him to shreds inside. He thought they were so much farther along, and now this? He knew she loved him still. He knew they had connected. Then she began to speak and broke into his thoughts.

"It's been very good and and—"

"Is this the way you want to end it?" he asked.

She stopped talking and looked at him with her mouth moving but no words coming out.

"It's not an end. It's—"

"This is me, Mel. Is this the way you want to end it?"

She took a step back and then looked away.

"I'm sorry you feel this way. I thought—"

"Mel," he whispered and it brought her head up right away. He couldn't keep the pain out of his voice.

"Calvin," she answered.

He walked up to her and threaded his hands into her hair and pulled her in for a long, deep kiss. When he pulled back, the both of them were breathing a little faster.

"I love you, Mel. I know I wasn't what you needed before but I'm here now, and I love you. You've grown so much and I'm so proud of you but you're going to have to trust me enough to take a chance on me again. There's nothing I can say to fix that or get you to the point. I'm leaving now, not because I want to, but you have to want us to be together again."

He turned and left out of the brownstone. He wasn't sure where he was going and it didn't even matter. Somehow he had managed to leave his heart in the brownstone but he was still moving. The only thing he could do now was wait and pray she'd be able to take that step.

Melinda hated to admit it but she needed her mother. It was crazy. In the grand scheme of things she had played a part in the crazy situation she was in. She had invited her mother other and had purchased her favorite dessert so they could have it with coffee or tea. Melinda was looking anxiously at the door until it rang. When it did she jumped off of the couch.

Melinda smiled and went to open the front door with a smile plastered on her face.

"Hi, Mom," she said, leaning in to give her a hug.

Beatrice raised an eyebrow and walked in. She had on blue jeans and a bright red tee shirt that had stenciled on it 'you wish you look this good when you get my age'.

Melinda wore a maxi dress with her hair up in a bun. It was a simple dress that she barely wore. She couldn't put on any makeup, but she did give herself a facial that claimed her skin would shine. She closed the door and watched her mother saunter into her home. She felt foolish thinking she was going to dress up and be more girly for her mother.

Melinda walked straight into her kitchen, spied the dessert box on the table, and then went to the Keurig to start some coffee.

"So you have to tell me what the problem is?" Beatrice asked.

"I picked up some desserts—"

"Yes my favorite, and you've decided to put on a dress."

Melinda stammered and looked around. The table was perfect, the dessert was right, what else could she give to her mom until she was ready?

"Stop, Melinda. You are thinking so much I'm getting tired. Let's go through the basics."

Melinda let out a sigh, gapped her legs open and then rested her hands in the well between her legs.

Beatrice pulled out two cups and talked over her shoulder.

"Okay, are you pregnant?"

"No!"

"Don't get in a huff. I'm just asking. I mean I'm your mother and you're a grown woman and it could happen."

"It doesn't just happen. At any rate, I'm not pregnant."

"Are you in any legal trouble?"

"No, mom. What is it that you think I do?"

Beatrice had two cups on the table and she had found the paper saucers to put on the table as well. She opened the box of desserts and smiled.

"It's not that I think you do a whole lot Melinda besides work and work and work. But you have to admit when your daughter goes all out to get your favorites and dresses for you, you have to start at the worst-case scenarios first."

Melinda rolled her hand on her leg.

"Okay, it's not that."

Beatrice sat down in the chair and took a bite of the cinnamon bun.

"Well then we're fine because that tells me is this is about a man, and since we all know what man is around, it's about Calvin."

Melinda gave up. She let her head fall on the table and told her tale of woe. When she was done she heard nothing. Melinda lifted her head and looked at her mom. Beatrice was looking at her with her mouth open.

"So, let me get this straight. You are this super emancipated woman who hasn't forgiven Calvin. Or are you the super emancipated woman who is too scared to try again?"

"You make everything sound so easy. It's not."

Beatrice held up her hand. "Hold on. Just give your mother a moment and listen. In the grand scheme of things, you can only do or not do. All that gray your generation says exists is not doing. So that being said, let's reduce this to our two options. You love this man and you're going to give it a try, or you love this man but not enough to forget your past."

Melinda stood up and shook her head. "You don't understand. I just—"

Melinda could feel the heat of tears in her eyes and she couldn't stop them from falling.

"Whoa, whoa! I have to tell you something. I love you. I don't judge because I'm in no position. I don't do tears. I'm not built that way. You have a problem. It's with Calvin, and you can't decide. So we have to do what women have done for centuries."

Melinda wiped the errant tears from her face and looked at her mom. "What would that be?"

"My child, so smart and sometimes you just miss the mark. It's called retail therapy."

"Mom."

"Shh, don't argue. I'm paying today, and you know that doesn't happen often. My opinion is you need to go get that man. But I know you are so full of feelings now. We'll buy stuff, we'll get some bad food and then come back and see how you feel then. Okay?"

Melinda nodded. Beatrice wasn't going to win any mother of the year awards but she was what Melinda needed for the now.

Melinda was in her living room and she was once again lost in between despair and fury. She understood that anger was the first emotion when an event happened. A person could stay angry for a very long time until they were ready to move on and examine their true feelings. She had gone through this process before when she and Calvin had broken up. However knowing the process academically didn't help at all when it came to dealing with the pain.

It was so funny to her that the one thing she was trying to avoid was the pain she had experienced before when she had broken up with Calvin. Now here she was again. In an attempt to avoid pain from him, she was in more pain than before.

Every day she came home, she felt stupid for thinking about a man who she was sure wasn't thinking about her. After the wave of silliness passed, then the gloom of sadness began that made her rethink everything and begin the crying binge. She thought she was past this cycle of useless crying and self-doubt. If anyone had asked her a couple of days ago, she would have said she had an internal strength that prevented her from falling into the pit of despair that she associated with failed relationships. The emancipated view she had of herself was slowing being decimated by the tear-swollen eyes that met her every morning.

She hadn't called Calvin in four days. She didn't want to admit it was her. She had spent a long time learning how to make decisions and stick with them. Certainly she wasn't going to throw that all away now. It would throw away all of the work she'd done. The fact that she'd already tried to work with Calvin was a big accomplishment. On most nights she could almost convince herself that she had done the best thing by walking away.

The problem was there was no peace in her decision. Instead of feeling free and liberated from Calvin and the memory of what they had, she felt alone. She felt like she had lost something that was special and unique. Pearla had given her several projects to choose from and had also asked her to give the write up on the brownstone project with Calvin. Now on her day off, she was trying to finish up the paperwork, and still, she wasn't able to shake Calvin or to find contentment with her decision.

At night it was the worst. She would lie in bed and wonder if Calvin was thinking about her. When the wind blew against her window she'd wonder if it was a knock on her front door. She would imagine that it was Calvin coming to say he loved her and wanted her, and just like in the movies, she would run into his arms and hug him and tell him she knew he'd come. The problem was when she looked outside the window, what she saw was a stray cat foraging in the garbage.

This go round the separation was different. It wasn't like the first time when she felt used and abandoned and had no sense of self. This time she felt as though she had lost a friend. She recalled the times they ate together, the times when she could bounce ideas off of him. It wasn't a dependent relationship with her rudder in life gone like the first time. This was more like she'd lost a buddy. Almost like losing Jasmine her bestie but in a guy form. The loss was deeper because it insinuated itself into her everyday life. When she saw something, she'd think, what would Calvin think? Or sometimes when she saw something on television it would bring up a shared memory that only the two of them would be able to laugh about. Yeah, missing Calvin was a whole new experience for her.

Jasmine had come over a couple of days ago. She had been waiting at her door. Melinda had let her into her apartment but nothing had really been resolved by the end of the night. Jasmine wanted to help her but Melinda wasn't ready to be helped and it made her feel like a heel with Jasmine. Eventually Jasmine left and she looked as despondent as Melinda.

It was her day off and she thought she could identify the problem. Calvin was now the full package and she could appreciate it. He was right. She was hedging her bets and not getting involved. Just as she was about to get some paper and write down the pros and cons of the situation her bell rang. Her heart picked up a beat and that hope like an ember was flaring in her chest. Was it Calvin?

"Open the door, Melinda."

Hope was replaced by despair.

"Mother?"

"Don't pretend you're not in there. I already checked at your job and they said you were going to be working from home for the next couple of days."

What was she doing here? The last thing she wanted to do was to deal with her mother. She dragged herself to pull open the door and tried to paste a smile on her face. If only she could dress and think quicker. If she had been faster, then she'd be able to come up with some story about her leaving to take care of something. That Beatrice had already called her job to find out her schedule didn't bode well. She was trying to think about what she was going to say, and before she could even open her mouth, her mother held up her hand.

"Don't even bother trying to tell me something that we both know isn't the truth. Thank goodness you were never any good at lying."

Beatrice brushed by as she entered into her place. As usual Beatrice looked amazing. She must be some part time senior model that got the best deals on the most flowy outfits. She had on a long maxi dress that hugged her as she walked. It was a beautiful peach and she wore sandals in a tan color. When Melinda looked at Beatrice's face she saw Beatrice had the look of someone who was about to lay down the law.

She was in the living room walking in circles. Then she stopped and took a breath.

"I'm curious. How long are you intending to sulk?" she asked as she found a seat and floated into the chair. All of the folds of her outfit just fluttered around her like a butterfly. Did she practice that move?

"I'm not sulking," she muttered.

"Oh no? Well, it appears you stayed with yourself too long and you've managed to talk yourself out of using your common sense. I had to show up because no one can seem to be able to talk to you. However, I knew that our relationship would help you see past this barrier that you have erected."

Melinda closed the door and turned to face Beatrice.

"There is nothing wrong with my common sense. I'm doing what I think is best. You were the one who told me I needed to care for myself and that is what I'm doing."

Beatrice just laughed. "Wow you kids are really good at coming up with stories to make yourselves sleep better at night."

The statement took the gusto out of her and she just walked over to her couch and plopped down.

"What do you want me to do?"

"Oh no young lady, it doesn't go that way. I came here to tell you, you were letting your doubts and fears run amuck. Now you may decide to let that keep happening and ignore everything I'm saying, but make no doubt, at the end of the day, it will be that you made a decision, not that I made it for you."

Melinda looked at Beatrice and took a deep breath. It was the worst when she discovered that Beatrice was right. Hadn't she been coming to this conclusion, that she wasn't the same and neither was Calvin? That maybe it was time to make a decision based on where they were right now and not based on where they were?

Beatrice snapped her fingers, and Melinda's head popped up. She licked her lips anxiously and then sank back into the couch.

"What have I done?"

Beatrice stood up. "Apparently not enough. I know you think I'm flighty and that I'm always going from one thing to another, and you might be right, but I have to tell you that it looks that way because I live in the moment and I don't hold onto the past. I've made my share of mistakes, but you have to make your peace with them or be buried with them."

Sitting up on the couch she wiped away an errant tear from her eye.

"I need to call him." As if the words gave Melinda some momentum, she got up, grabbed her phone, and called him.

The phone rang and rang. After the third ring it went to voicemail.

"This is Calvin, sorry I missed your call. I've started

on a new project. I should be back in a week but I'll be checking my messages periodically. If you have an emergency please call Nathan at 346 555 1212."

She hung up the phone and with it came a wave of disbelief.

"You didn't leave a message?"

Melinda hung up the phone and called the HR Director, Kida.

"Kida I'm sorry to call you at home but I have a question. Do you know about my mentee leaving?"

"Melinda? Yes, I do. I got the notice from him yesterday and I haven't had a chance to process it yet. I thought I had some time because the last project was completed and he hadn't been assigned to a new one yet in the system."

Melinda could hear Kida's apprehension.

"It's no problem. I just contacted him to make sure he had followed the protocol and was gone."

Kida's voice lightened up and it was a little more chipper.

"Oh no he was very thorough. He handed in all of his gear, ID, and property with the copies he had done for the site. I wish everyone was that organized."

Melinda nodded, but the only thing she could really hear was that he was gone. When she hung up Beatrice was standing with her arms crossed.

"Okay, what's wrong?"

Melinda put her cell phone down and shook her head.

"He left," she said in a low voice.

Beatrice sighed. "Well, it's not a good position to be in but did he leave a number?"

Melinda heard Beatrice's words through a haze of hurt.

"How could he leave and not even tell me?"

Beatrice grabbed Melinda by the forearms. "Melinda pull yourself together. You can call him and—"

Melinda stepped out of Beatrice's reach.

"Call him? He left me."

"Melinda he hasn't left you. He left so you could figure out what you were doing."

Melinda shook her head. "No!"

"Melinda?" Beatrice said reaching for her.

"No, that's not what this is and you don't see that he left me because you think I should be grateful to be with him. You think I should be happy that he wants anything to do with me and—"

Beatrice took one step back, blinked, and interrupted her with a quiet tone. "Melinda Sarah Tavers!"

Melinda stood stock still. That force and hearing her full name had the effect of stopping her in her tracks. Melinda waited. She'd never seen Beatrice like this. It was a combination of hurt and anger.

Beatrice straightened her back and blinked a couple of times before she spoke.

"Now hear me, Melinda. No matter what you think, you have always been my pride and joy. You probably think I'm too much in your life, that I intervene too much, but I'm speaking to you as a person who had neither parent speak to her when she was growing up. They never attended my graduation. They never attended a game or an award ceremony. When I was eighteen I asked them why and their answer was they fed me and clothed me so they loved me. I never wanted you to doubt that I loved you Melinda. Now maybe that didn't come across the way it should have but I've never thought less of you. You are a gift to any man. I think I have to live the way I want you to live and I try. I live hard and fully every day. I love you but I won't lie to you. Calvin is a fine man and you are an equally fine woman but you don't like to show it. It doesn't make him the cat's meow and you less but I won't lie to you either. You need time to get past this hurt that's clouding your vision and I need time to get past that dagger you decided to throw at my heart."

Beatrice stood up and walked out the door.

Melinda watched her go and flinched when the door closed. Then after looking aimlessly around her living room she fell to her knees, dropped her head into her hands and cried.

Sixteen

"I want to thank you for accepting my invitation and coming back, Calvin," Pearla said from behind her oak desk in her office. She was just down the hall from Melinda. A Melinda that hadn't called him during the week he'd been away. However, he could tell she had tried his number at least five times while he was away if his caller ID could be trusted.

"Please, it wasn't a problem. You helped me earlier and I appreciate the opportunity you gave me to reconnect with a side of my business that I was a little too distant from."

"Yes, I will say that you left an impression here. So much so I wanted to talk to you about a future relationship with the company."

He sat back in the chair and relaxed. He didn't want to jump up for joy yet. He hadn't heard the conditions. What Calvin would have told anyone was the five caller ID hits from Melinda had him in a better mood than he thought he would be. When he left and he hadn't heard anything, he had beat himself up for pushing her too hard. After he returned and saw the caller IDs he knew it was only a matter of time. Calvin couldn't wait to see Melinda again.

"Calvin," Pearla said. "I've asked you here to find out if you would be interested in a consulting position with us. I know you have your own company and investments but it doesn't look like you are involved in their day to day operations. Of course there would be an NDA and a BAA agreement for confidentiality and a legal formality."

She reached over to the far side of her desk and pulled out a manila folder, which she passed to Calvin. He opened it and flipped through the pages until it specified the type of work and who he would have to answer to. He looked up and knew he had a smile on his face.

Pearla spoke. "Beyond you being an invaluable asset I happen to think that time heals most things. I'm hoping that is the case for you as well."

Calvin nodded. "I'm of the same mind. To add to it, I want you to know that I am excited to be doing the work."

"Excellent," Pearla said. "In this situation we can both be helpful to the other party."

"There are a lot of reports I'd like to see and some—"

Pearla interrupted him. "I appreciate your enthusiasm but please remember Calvin you are part of a team and it is that team lead that will have those requests."

Calvin smiled and held his hands up. "Occupational hazard, I'll wait to confer with my colleague."

"Speaking of your colleague. I haven't mentioned this arrangement to Melinda yet. I didn't see the point if you didn't accept. I try to do things with the least amount of drama. As soon as I get all of the papers signed and notarized as indicated on each sheet then I'm more than happy to update Melinda."

"That's great and thank you."

"Don't worry about being grateful or thanking me. I expect a solid day's work out of everyone."

They shook hands and he left Pearla's office. As he sat in his car he leaned his head back against the headrest and let out a big breath. He needed the time away to apply what he had learned and give a new perspective to projects. Now that he was back he knew half of his issue was addressed. However, he was still waiting for the important part of this plan to come together.

He was still waiting on Melinda to understand they were meant to be together again.

Melinda had a box of cinnamon pastries in her hands. She was standing on the doorstep of her mother's house. Beatrice owned a house that she rented out most of the time but Melinda knew when Beatrice wasn't feeling her best she would escape into the rental to get away. Melinda knew it was time to see her because over the last three days she had tried to reach out and apologize to her but was blocked.

First she called her on the phone and found out Beatrice had blocked her number. Then on the next day she tried to contact her on Facebook. On Beatrice's Facebook page she had changed her page banner with the words that said 'Rent-a-mother available'. Finally, she sent a private message to her and Melinda got a message from Facebook that said Beatrice had unfriended her.

Melinda heard the footsteps coming to the door and she held up the box so it would be seen via the door camera. The door opened and Melinda lowered the box.

"I want to grovel," Melinda said. Melinda looked at Beatrice standing in the doorway. She had to admire that no matter what happened to Beatrice she had an indomitable spirit. Melinda hoped that as she got older she would have at least half the strength Beatrice had. Until recently Melinda hadn't considered how strong Beatrice was and how having that example in her life had given her the courage to find herself away from Calvin. With the good and inspirational also came challenges. Beatrice was a force and when she did something she did it unapologetically. She had an opinion and kept to it. That steadfastness could easily become stubbornness. That was how she explained her stubborn behavior. Melinda hoped the other attributes would transfer to her sooner rather than later.

Beatrice took the box and turned to go into the house and Melinda sighed. Melinda closed the door and walked into the sitting room. The room was a square and sported large windows, a high-backed chair that Beatrice was sitting in, with a loveseat on the side. Melinda sat on the loveseat with her fingers clasped together. She waited for Melinda to finish the first cinnamon Danish before she continued.

Beatrice swallowed and Melinda jumped in.

"I shouldn't have said those things to you. I was hurt and I wanted some pity and you weren't giving it so I made you the easy enemy."

Beatrice had picked up a napkin and wiped her hands

and put the box on the side. Melinda could see Beatrice wasn't saying a word and she was getting nervous that whatever she did may never be enough.

"I didn't know what you had done or how you'd grown up. We never talked about the details. We always seem gloss over it. What I really mean to say is that I am sorry." Melinda heard the words echo in the room and even she had to admit that the words felt hollow but at this point it was all she could do.

"Thank you."

Melinda stopped when she heard Beatrice speak. It wasn't the conversation she hoped for, in fact she had hoped her confession would have encouraged something more and the fact that it didn't was making her nervous.

"I know that it's not really enough for me to be sorry and to apologize. I see now that I damaged something special because I was being childish and I'm hoping that I can work my way back. I need to know if—"

Beatrice held up one hand.

"You're my daughter. I love you. I love you when you act poorly and I'll always love you. You don't have to worry about me not being in your life. I can accept who you are but I have to tell you trusting that person is not the same thing. I need time to trust."

"Fair enough," Melinda said.

"So you're here with me. Did you decide about Calvin?"

Melinda nodded. "Calvin met with my boss. If he sends in the paperwork he'll be back."

Beatrice smiled. "So you have a second chance with him as well?"

"I hope so. I haven't actually talked to him yet so I can't say one way or another," Melinda said while looking away for something else, anything else to focus on.

"So what are you going to do?"

Melinda gave a wan smile.

"Well, my thought was that if the groveling thing worked with you, then I could try it with him," she said looking to Beatrice to give an answer.

"I don't know much about groveling, but I do know a lot about making a statement and impressing someone. Will you let me help you?"

Melinda smiled. "I thought you would never ask."

Seventeen

Calvin was doing his best to keep a straight face at the table. Melinda pushed away from the table and went into the kitchen.

"Oh, I forgot two things. Stay here," Melinda said.

Calvin was sitting at the table in Melinda's place, looking at the meal that had been laid before him. The dishes were an array of hopeful dishes that had at one time had a lot of potential but someone let Melinda touch it.

Melinda had tried several times when they were together, but cooking was one of the things she had never been able to master. However, looking at the effort that she had gone through for him, he was impressed.

Melinda came out of the kitchen with a bowl of what looked like dressing for a salad. After she had placed the saucer on the table, she looked at him with a large smile.

"I put vinegar and oil in the saucer if you want some. It would take up too much room to put both bottles. I mean it's not like they were going to stay together anyway."

"I see," Calvin said.

Melinda had a smile on her face and then she straightened up and smiled. "Well at least the rest of it made it to the table."

Calvin looked at the assortment of food and wasn't even sure where to start.

"I didn't know you had taken up a renewed interest in cooking," he said trying to find a way out of having to eat what was on the table or at the very least having to eat the least toxic item.

"Yes, I have been cooking again. Since I was single, I had to do for myself."

Melinda picked up the salad bowl and offered it to Calvin. "I know the salad is a little wilted. I forgot how sensitive salad could be. I mean I put it on the stove for a few moments while I cleaned up, and when I took it off of the pot, it was already wilting," she complained.

"I hate when that happens to me," he said nodding his head vigorously to stop himself from laughing out loud. "I am truly moved and impressed by you inviting me over for dinner. I thought we were going to do something else when you said dinner."

"No, I wanted you to see I can take risks," Melinda said. "You know it's not always very evident how people try new things but I think it's important that people do.

Calvin grinned. "I'm a firm believer that risk taking is definitely worth it if the end goal is worthy."

Melinda smiled. "Great, I'm glad we are on the same page." She reached over to the fried chicken plate and when she tried to grab the chicken with the tongs the chicken fell back to the plate and the skin came off.

"Ugh! I'm so sorry. I wanted to keep the chicken warm because it had been finished first. I didn't put that much water on it but it seems like something was probably wrong with the flour and that's why the skin isn't sticking. It's not a problem. I'll take the skin off and we'll move on. Who wants the skin anyway? I hear it's unhealthy."

Calvin watched her strip the skin from the chicken and then put it on his plate. The good news was he could tell the chicken was completely cooked. Then she dropped a couple of wilted leaves on his plate. Lastly, she opened up a closed container and picked up a serving spoon. Inside of the floral Corningware was rice. She scooped it up and when she brought it to his plate it wouldn't leave the spoon. Finally, she picked up the tongs and pushed the sticky ball of rice onto his plate.

"It's good timing that you wanted to meet for dinner. As I'm sure you know Pearla has offered me a consulting space at the company."

"Oh yes, I think you deserve it. It will give you a chance to settle in the area, and you know, do some settling," she said.

Calvin nodded and then he noticed that Melinda was sitting with some food on her plate, but she hadn't touched a thing. It came to him he was going to have to eat something here. He put on a wider smile and then cut into the chicken and put it into his mouth. He kept chewing when the salty meat hit his tongue and maintained his smile as he swallowed.

"Do you like it? It was in soy sauce all day long to give it flavor."

"It's a new flavor for me."

Melinda nodded and then cut a piece of the chicken and then took a bite before making a face of utter disgust. "Oh my, this is horrible," Melinda exclaimed.

"It's a little salty but this is definitely something you could use for people with a cold."

Melinda gave him a side eye of disbelief. She then used her tongs to dig into the salad bowl. When she put her tongs down and tried to pick up the salad with the tongs, the leaves were too wilted.

Calvin interrupted her by clearing his throat, making her look up and then using his own fork to demonstrate how to accomplish the task.

"You need to use the fork like a scoop or shovel. Don't try to pierce it, scoop it."

Melinda looked at her plate and then looked at Calvin demonstrate the task. He scooped the leaf and ate it. Melinda followed suit.

The first chew her face was tense. "This salad is pretty bad."

"Now Melinda—"

"Calvin please, don't bother trying to fix this I wouldn't feed this to people I don't like, much less someone I care for."

She sounded so forlorn. He reached over and rubbed her back.

"Mel, this had never been a strong point for you. It will just take time."

Melinda shook her head as she hung it in shame. "I had Jasmine make all the food and it was great. I ate when she finished and it was great. Somehow I put too much of everything when I tried to heat it up. I tried to clean the kitchen so I piled all the food on the stove and it melted."

"I want you to know that I appreciate this so much and I appreciate you."

Melinda sat back and eyed him for a moment.

"Did Beatrice give you a call today, besides asking you to come to my house?"

Calvin turned from her and looked at the table. The concept of trying something was making his stomach cramp before he even tasted anything.

"Calvin! Tell me the truth."

"Well she said that it was very important that I have patience tonight because—"

"She told you I wanted us to get together, didn't she?"

Calvin reached out to touch Melinda's hand and she pulled it back.

"Why oh why can't she let me do things my way?"

Calvin held up his hands. "She was concerned is all. She told me that you might be open to a relationship now and that it would be in my best interest to go to dinner with you tonight."

Melinda groaned. "I should have known better when she said she had a plan. I told her I wasn't sure about this and ugh! It is what it is. So that only leaves your answer Calvin. What's it going to be? Are you going to be with me or not?"

"Excuse me?" Calvin said. He certainly could not have heard her correctly.

"Come on Calvin. I tried to do this and it was a total cluster but I want an answer."

He couldn't help but smile at her impatience. "I would be happy to answer the question if you could be a little clearer. I mean are you asking if I'm going to be with you at work or—"

"First of all get that smug look off of your face you know exactly what I'm talking about. Are you going to be with me in a relationship again or what?"

Calvin picked up the napkin off of the table and dabbed at his mouth. "I have to say I don't feel like this was the most romantic offering ever."

Melinda threw up her hands. "Romance! Do you know how long poor Jasmine slaved in that kitchen only to have me destroy the end result? It's not about romance that comes and goes. It's about the work. What's important is for you to know that I'm willing to do the effort it takes to make sure we work. The fact that I think you're worth all this effort should be something."

Calvin stood up and pulled her up into his arms as she stood.

"You did real good Mel."

Melinda tried to wave off his comments.

"Listen you don't' have to patronize me or lead me down the path gently. Just let me know."

"There's no doubt that my answer is yes."

He could see Melinda gearing up to speak and then she stopped short.

"Really?"

"Yes, love. I want to note just for later review that you can't ever say that I don't listen. I've been telling you from the very beginning that I want you and I wanted us to be together."

She blinked and looked at him for a moment before speaking.

"I want to hear it again."

Calvin smiled and leaned down and placed a kiss on her cheek.

"I want to be with you." He leaned down and kissed her other cheek. "I want to be your partner in life."

She smiled and then leaned her forehead against his. "I was scared."

He lifted her chin up so they were gazing into each other's eyes.

"You were courageous, beautiful and bold. I was humbled by this whole event," he whispered as he leaned down to kiss her. He took his time. Calvin kissed her slowly and deeply. When he lifted his head, his breath was quicker, and his hands had tightened on her waist.

"I know you left because you needed to find yourself and embrace the strong woman that you are, but I'm glad you came back because without you I was incomplete. I love Melinda, welcome back."

"I love you too Calvin, it's good to be together again."

Epilogue

Lionel sat in the back of the room watching the party in the diner. It was odd for his friend Michael to host his engagement party here. Lionel guessed when men were in love they did odd things.

Lionel trusted numbers and probability. Everything else was too chaotic for him. He watched Michael and Cora dance, twirling each other around on the floor. He could think of only one person who would even think about twirling on the floor. Her name was Fiona Dunn. He wasn't sure she would even remember him but she was the standard he had carried with him since he was eighteen.

This party was like so many other parties he had been to. He was in the party but not a part of the party. Every now and again a woman would smile at him. The only thing he could think of was how the young lady's smile didn't compare to Fiona.

Over the years he had looked back at Rolling Springs to see how she was doing. She hadn't left Rolling Springs like he thought she would but it didn't matter she still flourished. She was the town treasurer now and a voice to be listened to in their old town.

She had been engaged twice but never married. Both times he had waited for the wedding to be announced. Lionel had decided if she found another he would stay with Aster, his cat and live out his days alone. Instead, both times she had been engaged and neither one had resulted in them making it to the altar. Lionel thought on it a while and decided the third time would be the charm.

He rose and looked at the crowd. No one stopped him as he went to the door. The valet outside of the restaurant took his ticket and drove his truck to the front. He knew the valet was confused looking at him in tailored clothes and then bringing out what could only be called an old jalopy. It was the same type of truck he had drove off in when he had left Rolling Springs as a teen. No matter how much money he made it helped him remember where he came from.

As he took his seat in the truck he made a realization. He was a lot like this truck, beaten, old and worn. Lionel couldn't remember the last time he had enjoyed anything like the people in the diner. If he kept this up he'd end up like this truck, an eyesore that eventually would be discarded.

He wanted to know what it would be like to twirl Fiona around the dance floor. He wanted Fiona to meet Aster. He wanted to share all that he was and had with Fiona. He always did the safe thing but tonight that would change.

Lionel started the engine and drove off. He was going to donate the truck and find a way to go get the woman he loved.

I hope you enjoyed Melinda and Calvin's story. If you'd like to read another second chance romance Check out *Forgive Me* for book five of the Love Endures series and read Lionel and Fiona's story.

Sign up to my newsletter to receive updates on new releases, sale promotions, and free books.

susanwarnerauthor.com